"Michael, there's no future in this,"

Blair said. "You know I'm attracted to you, but I don't want to be. It wouldn't work, and it has nothing to do with you or your job. It has to do with me and who I am."

"Why are you complicating things?" he murmured, a small smile beginning to light his eyes. "I thought this was about an invitation to a wedding?" He shifted one hand to stroke his thumb along her jawline.

She found herself leaning into his touch. "I'm not trying to complicate it. You are. Don't tempt me, Michael. I don't want to disappoint you."

"Ask me once more," he said, his dark gaze wandering over her features as if he were a sculptor about to immortalize her in marble. "Let me take you to the wedding."

Say no, her mind shouted at her. *It won't work. He'll break your heart, or you'll break his. You don't have time for this!*

But more than anything, she wanted to feel his mouth again.

"Yes," she managed, her throat desperately dry. "Please."

Dear Reader:

All of us here at Silhouette Books hope that you are having a wonderful summer, and enjoying all that the season has to offer. Whether you are vacationing, or spending the long, warm summer evenings at home, we wish you the best—and hope to bring you many happy hours of romance.

August finds our DIAMOND JUBILEE in full swing. This month features *Virgin Territory* by Suzanne Carey, a delightful story about a heroine who laments being what she considers "the last virgin in Chicago." Her handsome hero feels he's a man with a mission—to protect her virtue *and* his beloved bachelorhood at the same time. Then, in September, we have an extraspecial surprise—*two* DIAMOND JUBILEE titles by two of your favorite authors: Annette Broadrick with *Married?!* and Dixie Browning with *The Homing Instinct*.

The DIAMOND JUBILEE—Silhouette Romance's tenth anniversary celebration—is our way of saying thanks to you, our readers. To symbolize the timelessness of love, as well as the modern gift of the tenth anniversary, we're presenting readers with a DIAMOND JUBILEE Silhouette Romance each month, penned by one of your favorite Silhouette Romance authors.

And that's not all! This month don't miss Diana Palmer's fortieth story for Silhouette—*Connal*. He's a LONG, TALL TEXAN out to lasso your heart! In addition, back by popular demand, are Books 4, 5 and 6 of DIANA PALMER DUETS—some of Diana Palmer's earlier published work which has been unavailable for years.

During our tenth anniversary, the spirit of celebration is with us year-round. And that's all due to you, our readers. With the support you've given us, you can look forward to many more years of heartwarming, poignant love stories.

I hope you'll enjoy this book and all of the stories to come. Come home to romance—Silhouette Romance—for always!

Sincerely,

Tara Hughes Gavin
Senior Editor

HELEN R. MYERS

Invitation to a Wedding

Silhouette Romance

Published by Silhouette Books New York

America's Publisher of Contemporary Romance

For Jane Larson,
who's eternally young at heart
Thanks for coming into my life.

SILHOUETTE BOOKS
300 E. 42nd St., New York, N.Y. 10017

ISBN: 0-373-08737-3

First Silhouette Books printing August 1990

HELEN R. MYERS

lives on a sixty-five-acre ranch deep in the piney woods of east Texas with her husband, Robert, and a constantly expanding menagerie. She lists her interests as everything that doesn't have to do with a needle and thread. When she and Robert aren't working on the house they've built together, she likes to read, garden and, of course, outfish her husband.

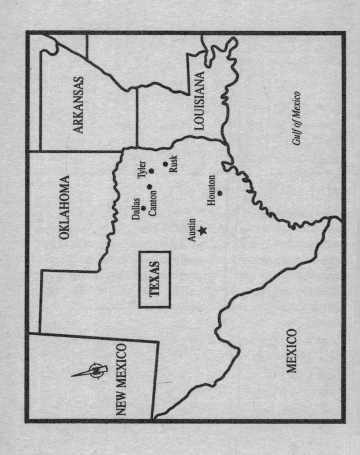

Chapter One

Have you found anyone yet?"

At the sound of her mother's voice on the other end of the telephone line, Blair Lawrence shot a glance at the man misting the dieffenbachia on her office coffee table and tensely tapped her pen against her desk blotter. Here we go again, she thought wearily, and what awful timing.

"No, not in the forty minutes since your last call, Mother," she replied, keeping her voice as low as possible. "And I thought I told you then that I don't have time to discuss *the matter*. I have a meeting in less than two hours and a presentation to finish."

Martha Lawrence clucked her tongue. "Blair, honey, you're always going to or coming from some meeting. How often does your only brother get married?"

"Give him time, he's only twenty-three."

"Why, that's a terrible thing to say. He and Alicia make a darling couple and anyone can see that they were made for each other. Anyway, I didn't call this time to talk about who you're bringing to the wedding, though I've started a list in case things don't work out on your end. I just wanted to tell you that I think I've got the catering problem taken care of after all. Wait until you hear this . . ."

Blair dropped the pen and with one hand covered her eyes. Once again she found herself wondering at the possibility that at her birth she'd been inadvertently switched with another baby in the hospital nursery. How could anyone get so preoccupied with plotting, planning and all-around meddling? Poor Alicia, maybe someone should warn her about what she was getting herself into.

At least Tim could be sure of his lineage; he'd inherited everything from their mother all the way down to his wiry build, crinkly blue-gray eyes and effusive disposition. Blair, with her thick mahogany hair and her somber brown eyes, couldn't even claim to look like one of their distant cousins. She knew who they all *said* she resembled, but she preferred to stick with the mix-up in the hospital theory.

Shifting her hand to rub her temple, she found that the quiet man she only knew as "Michael" had paused in his chores and was eyeing her over the rims of his aviator-style glasses with a mixture of curiosity and concern. Giving him a weak smile, she swung her executive chair around to face the window that ran the length of her office and looked out over Dallas's Thanksgiving Square. Great, she fumed inwardly, even the corporate plant man could tell her mother was driving her batty.

Why couldn't Tim and Alicia have simply eloped while on their way to Tim's new public relations job in California? As much as she loved her younger sibling, it was difficult to muster the same enthusiasm as everyone else over the couple's sudden decision to have a June wedding. Not that her mother couldn't organize one in four weeks; the problem was, in her usual steamroller fashion, she was also determined to organize Blair's life in the process.

"No, you're absolutely right, children won't eat it if it's too spicy. It's better to stick with the mild sauce," she told her mother.

Out of the corner of her eye she could see that Michael had moved on to the weeping fig tree. It was thriving under his thorough care. He misted, polished and pampered as if he were a doctor treating a patient, she thought, shifting to watch him use a leaf polish and a soft cloth to heighten the luster on some dulled foliage. Despite his obvious talent, it struck her as a waste for someone who seemed to have such intelligent eyes. Heaven only knew what possessed some people to choose the occupations they did.

"That sounds fine. Mom—"

Her secretary, Tess Reed, walked in with the cup of tea she'd ordered minutes before. Tess's eyes lit up when she saw Michael and they exchanged whispered greetings. Feeling a renewed sense of peevishness, Blair swung back to the window; terrific, she thought, now her office was turning into a lounge.

Even though Michael left moments later, Blair decided she'd had enough. "Mom...Mother, I have to cut this short. My boss is on the other line. If you think the centerpiece is going to clash with the colors Alicia's chosen, then by all means call her and take it up with her... That's right... What?... Yes, I'll call as soon as my own plans are settled. Bye."

While Blair placed the red phone receiver back onto its cradle, Tess carefully set the black china cup and saucer on her desk blotter, asking, "What's that make it, third time this morning?"

"Fourth. That's not counting the wake-up call I got at five this morning when it hit her that I hadn't mentioned who I was bringing to the blissful event." Blair glanced around her secretary to make sure Michael was gone, or at least out of earshot. "If she calls again, and you value your boss's sanity, tell her I'm out, in a meeting, whatever."

Tess sat down on the arm of one of the upholstered chairs that matched the black and red color scheme in the office and nodded solemnly. "Drink your tea. You'll feel better."

"Only if it's laced with cyanide."

Humor brightened her secretary's honey-brown eyes. In an attempt to smother it she concentrated on smoothing the skirt of her red plaid jumper. "What was it this time, did the caterer balk at the idea of serving chicken-fried steak at the reception?"

"Oh, we're way past that." Blair decided she no longer wanted the tea and opened the top drawer of her desk to hunt down her roll of antacids. "You know my mother, Martha the Manipulator—whatever she wants, she gets." Belatedly she remembered she'd eaten the last one yesterday after being turned down in her third attempt at finding an escort to accompany her to the wedding. Shaking her head she shut the drawer and reached for the tea after all.

"It was bad enough that she talked Tim and Alicia into moving the wedding from the third to the second Saturday in June," she continued. "Remember I told you about that? The third Saturday is the anniversary of Aunt Violet finding out Uncle Monroe was seeing that waitress in Fort Worth. Mom didn't want to be disrespectful to Violet, even though it's been seventeen years. Now she's decided that chicken-fried steak isn't exotic enough for a wedding reception. She's hired Mr. Perez at Tio Paco's Café and Cantina, who's assured her that not only can he have a mini-taco shell created especially for her, but that a swan centerpiece made out of frozen guacamole isn't beyond his chef's capabilities."

Tess lifted her fingers to her lips. "Oh, dear. You're going to have to take pictures of that one."

"Why don't I just have Mother send you an invitation?"

"I couldn't possibly go," her secretary replied with a shake of her head that sent her naturally curly blond hair bouncing. "I think Neiman Marcus is having a ten percent off hosiery sale that weekend."

Blair eyed her glumly over the tea cup. "Go ahead and make jokes. Only remember this great show of support when it comes time to do your next six-month review."

With a deep sigh Tess rose and walked over to close the office door. "Okay. What's really behind all this—and don't tell me it's your mother's weird ideas about this wedding and how she had to fill you in on every little detail. If she didn't call about that, she'd call about the farm, your infrequent visits or this week's *National Enquirer* headlines. After almost two years of screening your calls, even *I* know better than to expect her to change. So what has you looking like you just lost your biggest account?"

Blair considered the young woman who, at twenty-six, was four years younger than her and once again thought how grateful she was that they'd developed a friendship beyond their solid professional relationship. She didn't have many female friends, there had never been time to cultivate them; having one who was so conveniently at hand was a double blessing.

Even so, it wasn't easy making her confession. In fact, as Blair found herself trying to put her plight into words, she found it was downright *embarrassing*.

"Blair."

"Oh, all right. I don't have a date." She grimaced at the term. "An escort, I don't have an escort. Of course, if it were up to me, it wouldn't matter—I don't see any great need to bring anyone, and I know it isn't something Tim's losing sleep over, either. But you know my mother."

"If she's even slightly suspicious, she's going to make a list of potential candidates to ask in your behalf."

"She's already started."

Tess sat down again and began thoughtfully scratching the area under her chin. "Well, your passport doesn't have to be renewed until October..."

"Please. Don't tempt me."

Putting down the cup Blair stood and went back to the window. Below in the square she saw city employees taking out tired-looking pansies and daffodils from the flower beds and replacing them with begonias, marigolds and caladiums. Soon the pebble and concrete retaining walls with their inlaid water chutes would be crowded with office workers snatching a few minutes of mid-May sun as they ate their sack lunches. She'd never indulged in the pastime herself.

Her demanding job didn't leave her with much time for friendships and romance, or for sitting in the park. Blair was one of the top ad executives at McGowan and Birch, one of Dallas's leading advertising firms. Although the achievement hadn't come easily, she never regretted paying the price. She loved her work, the challenge and creativity involved in taking a customer's product or service and working up a campaign that would show it off to its fullest potential. Having grown up in an environment where every penny had to be counted in order to make ends meet, Blair enjoyed the financial rewards and security her work gave her.

She'd never even thought to complain that the job left her with minimal time for dating. Her work required more than enough socializing to satisfy her, and in the nine years she had been in the business, she'd established several friendships with men who could be relied upon to serve as appropriate escorts. Naturally she returned the favor in kind whenever she could, but she made it perfectly clear the accommodating stopped there. She wasn't interested in anything deeper. As a child—beginning the day her father had walked out—she'd learned that the cost of loving just wasn't worth the heartache.

But what was she supposed to do now that her trusty group of escorts had let her down?

"Wait a minute," Tess said reassuringly. "I know Elliot is out of the picture since he took the job offer in New York. But what about John?"

"He's going to be in Austin lobbying some project or other in behalf of the mayor."

"Walt?"

"He says he's already asked to have the kids that weekend and they have special plans lined up." Blair came back to sit on the edge of her desk and nodded at Tess's look of skepticism. "Yeah, that's what it sounds like to me, too. Only Seth, bless his heart, had the guts not to lie to me. After the experience of taking my mother and me out to dinner he told me he'd rather take a water-tasting trip through Mexico." Feeling a new surge of embarrassment, Blair fingered one of her gold geometric-shaped earrings. "Now I know what an unsold Christmas tree feels like on December twenty-sixth."

Tess uttered a sound of frustration and, rising, grabbed her hand to lead her to the coat closet. Opening it, she placed Blair before the full-length mirror that had come with the office. "Will you look at yourself? You're gorgeous, young and successful. What else do you want?"

Blair frowned at her reflection. She'd stopped paying more than haphazard attention to her looks while she'd still been in college. By then she'd resigned herself to the fact that at five foot nine she was always going to tower over most of her friends and that with her curvy figure, she was never going to look like what the fashion magazines said was *in*.

Still, she knew she had a certain something...a strong classical look that needed only the simplest attention to give her a casual sort of sophistication. Thus, she kept her thick, mahogany brown hair in a blunt chin-length cut and her wardrobe centered around equally dramatic colors like black, red, navy and white.

She considered the black jersey sheath with the wide soft leather belt resting on her hipbones and wondered if, after four years, it wasn't beginning to show its age. For that matter, was she? Thirty might be nothing when considering she was the youngest executive in the firm, but in the past few weeks, specifically since Tim had announced his engagement, she was beginning to feel the sands of time weighing down on her shoulders.

"What do I want?" she repeated, scowling into the mirror as if it were a crystal ball. "I want my mother to stop meddling in my life. I want Tim and Alicia to elope. I *want* to be able to feel that it's not the end of the world if I show up at the wedding without a man in tow."

She lifted her gaze to Tess.

"Better find a date," they declared in unison.

"The only problem is there's no one left to ask," Blair added. Granted, there were one or two of her associates here at the office who she knew would welcome an invitation to go out with her, but she didn't want to send out the wrong kind of signal. Defeated, she headed back to her desk to finish her tea.

Giving her a sympathetic look, Tess shut the door. At the coffee table she leaned over to straighten the magazines. "Well," she said, also shifting the dieffenbachia to a better angle, "if worse comes to worst, I have this cousin. He's on the short side but—"

When she didn't finish, Blair glanced over her shoulder and saw she was standing there staring at the plant as if it had just sprouted a new leaf before her eyes. "But what?"

"Forget it. I just got a better idea, and I don't know why I didn't think of him before because he's perfect." Tess gave Blair a bright smile. "Ask Michael Bishop."

"And who, pray tell, is Michael Bishop?"

Tess pointed meaningfully at the dieffenbachia. "Michael Bishop."

"The plant man?" Cup and saucer clattered in Blair's hands. She set them back on her desk. With an embarrassed laugh she turned back to Tess. "You're not serious? This is the first time I've even heard his full name. I can't go out with a perfect stranger. Tell me more about this cousin of yours. Just how short is short?"

"He's a jockey."

Any minute now, Blair assured herself, she was going to wake up and discover that all this was a bad dream. What had she eaten last night while reviewing the Raven Cosmetics portfolio? No, cottage cheese on celery couldn't possibly be considered too heavy for the stomach.

"Tess, don't you understand? I can't take someone whose chief preoccupation in life is looking for spider mites to my brother's wedding. Don't get me wrong, I know that sounds incredibly snobbish and I don't mean to be. If he's happy at what he's doing, more power to him. But my relatives see me as this—success story. I have an image to sustain. Elliot's a corporate attorney...Seth teaches at SMU...Walt's an investment broker...that's the kind of man they'll expect me to bring. If I did ask Michael Bishop to go, what would we talk about? Root rot?"

"And just who do you think your mother will have on her list? The mayor of Fort Worth?"

In her mother's rural neighborhood the nearest small town had a Dairy Queen, a Mom and Pop grocery and a few other individually-owned businesses. Horace Breedlove was the community's undertaker and ever since his wife passed away, her mother had been dropping hints about him as weighty as her homemade biscuits. Blair barely suppressed a shudder.

"Michael and I have hardly done more than exchange greetings and comments about the weather," she reminded Tess.

"He's got a great body and a yummy smile."

And enigmatic eyes, Blair thought with a slight frown. More than once she'd been in the hallway, or down in the lobby, only to look up and see him watching her. She couldn't deny the experiences had left her wondering what he was thinking. Of course, that was the thing about quiet people; they always gave the impression of being mysterious when in fact, they were for the most part, simply shy.

"He's about as exciting as yogurt," she said stubbornly.

"Did I suggest you propose to him?"

That reminded Blair of something else. "What if he's already married?"

"Nope. I asked once."

Blair chuckled. "You would. I swear there isn't an inhibited bone in your body." But as quickly as her humor appeared, it vanished and she was left nibbling on her lower lip. Now what? She'd used up all her arguments and the strange thing was that the more she thought about it, the more she could see the logic of the suggestion. No one else need know she was inviting Michael Bishop, and he could be made to understand that this was a one-time only arrangement. The lack of external complications certainly appealed to her.

"Why don't you go ask him now while he's still in the building," Tess suggested, seeing she was considering the idea.

Blair glanced over at her work-laden desk. "I don't know, I still have a lot to do before that luncheon meeting. Why don't I wait until Friday and ask him when he comes to check the plants again?"

"Sure, you can sit behind that desk like you were Queen Elizabeth interviewing a vassal for the head-hankie-holder job. Come on, Blair, give the poor guy a break. Meet him on neutral ground. You can probably catch him down the hallway somewhere. Anyway, if you wait until the end of the week, who knows, he might already have plans.'' Just then the phone began to ring. Tess glanced from it to her boss. ''That could be your mother again.''

It was the final push Blair needed to galvanize her into action. ''All right, all right, I'm going,'' she muttered, jumping to her feet and rushing out the door.

But once out the front door of McGowan and Birch her confidence faltered sharply. She felt like an idiot. What was she going to say? What was he going to say? If he laughed, she vowed she was going to replace every live plant in her office with a silk one, because there was no way she was ever going to be able to face him again.

However, when she realized he wasn't anywhere on the fifth floor, Blair stopped worrying about his response to her invitation and began to wonder what to do next. Talk about fast workers, where was he? Could he already have finished here and moved up to the next floor?

''Hi, Blair. Something the matter?''

She spun around and gave McGowan and Birch's office manager a bright smile. ''Doug. No, I was only—ah—looking for Michael. I was going to ask him to—to suggest another plant for the coffee table in my office. It's getting so big, it really needs to be replaced.'' She almost winced hearing herself babble on, but apparently Doug didn't notice.

"Michael . . . is that his name? Guess I never paid much attention. I just saw him up on six. I think he was going into one of the consulates."

Blair thanked him and hurried to the elevators. Lovely, she told herself pushing the Up button. Now not only did she have the chore of inviting Michael Bishop to her brother's wedding, but she had to order another plant as well. And why hadn't she asked *which* consulate? There were several consulates in their building; three were on the sixth floor.

Moments later, as she exited the elevator, she found herself smoothing a hand over her hair. She'd never been to any of the consulates. Occasionally she saw one of the officials in the lobby or elevators. For the most part they looked like any other businessman in a three-piece suit carrying an attaché case. But she had to admit there was something exotic in the idea of being an international diplomat, even though she'd read Graham Greene's *The Honorary Consul* and Malcolm Lowry's *Under the Volcano* and knew her perception was nothing more than romantic illusion. Romantic . . . an odd word for a dyed-in-the-wool realist like herself.

The three consulates on the sixth floor all represented Latin American countries. As she attempted a casual walk by the plate-glass front window of one, she nodded to the receptionist inside. The young woman's coal black hair was conservatively wound in a tight bun at her nape. Her white blouse and brown skirt were equally severe. The woman's appearance seemed, somehow, at odds with the image of a country that had given the world so much of its flamboyance and color, Blair mused. But then what had she expected, parrots and flamenco dancers?

Shaking her head, she refocused on finding Michael. After walking down one hallway, she crossed over to the other side of the building to check the next one. Not only did she not find him, but upon her second pass in front of the second consulate's door, she caught the attention of an onyx-eyed Lothario who stepped outside to offer his assistance.

"Do you speak English?" she asked as he smiled deep into her eyes.

He gave her an apologetic shrug and brought his thumb and index finger together to signify a small portion. "I am, how you say—student."

"Wonderful, you're doing fine. Could you tell me if you've seen the corporate plant man around anywhere? The—" She sighed at his look of confusion and began to pantomime pouring a watering can. "Water, comprende?" *Or is it comprendo? Oh, God, how did I get myself into this?*

"Water! *Sí, señorita*, you are thirsty, yes? *Por favor.* You come inside for *café*."

"No! No, thank you so much—er, *gracias*, mucho. I'll just—oh, look, the ladies' room." She pointed to the door at the end of the hall. "I'll just go in there."

Thanking him again, she all but ran down the hall, slipped inside and then slumped back against the door.

This was getting ridiculous, she told herself. The man probably thought she was a nut case. She would be lucky if he didn't call building security—or did consulates have their own security? Wouldn't that just top everything if she were dragged back to McGowan and Birch in the tow of some Central American version of a KGB agent?

Shaking her head, she went to a sink and splashed cool water over her hands and wrists. Only when she thought enough time had lapsed for her mustached admirer to have gone away did she ease out of the rest room and start back down the hallway.

She decided she'd had enough. If she could just slip past his consulate without being seen, she could run to the elevators and get back downstairs. She had to have been crazy in the first place to let Tess talk her into this.

Flattened against the wall, she eased closer to the plate-glass window of the consulate, then carefully peered around the edge to look inside. There was a huge potted palm in the corner. Nearly sighing with relief, she crouched down to use it as a cover and peered between the fronds.

Whew...he was gone. Nice wallpaper, Blair noted, eyeing the kaleidoscope print in shades of blue and green.

"Blair? Is that you?"

She almost screamed. Only air locked in her throat stopped her; only quick thinking made her recover enough to grab her ankle and fiddle with the chain strap on her expensive high-heeled sandals. Peeking out from behind the veil of her hair, she saw the stuff of which nightmares are made. Michael Bishop standing by the elevators watching her.

"Michael—hello." Having always refrained from calling him anything, she found this first attempt at familiarity awkward, compounded by her total humiliation at being caught in this predicament. "Excuse me a moment. It's these shoes. Sometimes the chain gets twisted and—there, that's better." She straightened and walked over to him, hoping he bought her story, knowing he would be a complete yo-yo if he did. "I'm glad I found you."

"You want me?"

Though the question was posed in all innocence, Blair found herself embarrassed at the sexual innuendo her mind conjured and, for the first time in the—how long was it?—six or so months since he'd been coming to care for her plants, she found herself reacting to him as woman to man.

For the first time she noticed that even in her three-inch heels, he stood another two or three inches taller, and that his lean but athletic body seemed made for fitted clothes like the jeans and black polo shirt he was wearing. The hint of finely toned muscles stretched the material at his thighs and his shoulders. His wasn't the body of a weight lifter, but maybe a tennis player, rower or . . . she imagined him jogging along the trails at White Rock Lake or Turtle Creek, his long limbs glistening in the sun as he kept a brisk but comfortable pace. It made her feel uncomfortably warm, despite the adequate air-conditioning.

Embarrassed again she dragged her gaze up to meet his and found that behind those gold-framed glasses, his dark eyes were actually a charcoal gray. They were also a little less enigmatic than usual because of the amusement she saw in their depths. Oh, misery, she thought, tempted to pry open the elevator doors and dive down the shaft; he *knew* she'd been peeking into the consulate.

That knowledge almost made her oblivious to the fact that his smile was indeed "yummy," as Tess had described, and it fit his long, angular face crowned by a head of luscious wavy chestnut hair. Almost, but not quite.

"Umm—you left my office before I could get off the phone," she began, needing to buy time in order to collect her thoughts. "I wanted to ask you something."

"You should have signaled me. I would have waited."

He braced one hand against the wall and the other on his hip. It was a perfectly casual pose. So why did she suddenly feel cornered? Why did he suddenly remind her of one of those guys she'd hired to do that sports car ad? And why, instead of a pleasant, not particularly memorable face, did she have to notice that it had a somewhat Byronic beauty—the forehead noble, the nose a bit sharp, the chin determined?

"Well, you have your work, too," she murmured, shrugging, "and it wasn't all that earth-shattering."

"Must have been important enough for you to have traced me up here."

Gotcha. His words, as well as his look, made Blair feel like a butterfly pinned to a piece of Styrofoam. She fingered the hammered gold pendant resting between her breasts, as if by lifting it she could draw out the pin and gain her freedom.

"Oh, it's silly really. I mean it could have waited until the next time you came around. I just wanted to ask you if you might—"

A middle-aged man came around a corner and pressed the Down button, giving them a polite nod and folding his hands before him to await the arrival of a car. Blair could have wept from frustration. The last thing she needed was an audience.

"Might what?" Michael prompted casually. Too casually?

"Er...might..." She swallowed against the dryness of her throat and glanced at the man who pretended to be oblivious to their conversation. "Actually, Michael, I thought you could tell me how I'd know if my amaryllis has blight."

He managed to keep a straight face and for that alone she could have kissed him.

"Your amaryllis?"

"A gift from my brother, so you can understand when I say I've grown very attached to it."

"Of course."

Straightening, Michael took off his glasses and pinched the bridge of his nose. Blair could see he was trying to figure out what was going on and silently willed the elevator to hurry. Wait until she got her hands on Tess...

"What does your plant look like?" he asked politely.

Blair stared at him. Murder, what *did* blight look like? She never paid attention to the plants at her apartment. When the dirt was dry she watered, when the plants died, she threw them out and bought new ones.

"Yellow . . . umm, droopy . . . and, ah—"

"Like it was rotting?"

Was this a trick question or was he really trying to be helpful? "Well . . ." Blair murmured, clasping and reclasping her hands.

"Tell you what, why don't you bring it in Friday and I'll have look at it. Diagnosing a plant's problems by hearsay is as dangerous as a doctor diagnosing a patient without an examination."

That's it, Blair thought. She couldn't take anymore. To her relief the elevator arrived and, when the man beside them looked at her questioningly and murmured, "Down?" she nodded eagerly.

"I have to get back downstairs, Michael, but thanks bunches." She quickly stepped into the car. "I really appreciate the help."

"You'll bring the plant Friday?" he asked, leaning over to keep her in his view as the doors began to slide closed.

"Sure. You bet. Bye."

Her smile held until the doors were completely closed. Then like a petunia that had given up its battle with the scorching Texas sun, she wilted against the back of the elevator.

"So how did it go?" Tess asked excitedly when, minutes later, Blair returned to her office.

She paused by her secretary's desk and gave her a long, measuring look. "Remind me to order a new plant for my coffee table and find out where in the world I can find a sick amaryllis by Friday.''

''A what?''

''Don't ask me to explain,'' Blair muttered, heading into her office. ''You wouldn't believe it.''

Chapter Two

Excellence at the Excelsior. The Excelsior—An experience in excellence. Too many Xs. How about elegance? The Excelsior—An experience in elegance." Blair grimaced and tossed pad and pencil onto her desk. "Now I sound as though I'm plugging a restaurant."

Slumping back in her chair, she checked her watch. Incredible, she thought. It was past eight. No wonder all her ideas were sounding flat to her.

She reached for the black ink drawing of The Piazza, her mall project to be built just east of DFW airport. She was still stuck on coming up with a suitable motto for the hotel that would be adjacent to the luxurious marketplace. Correction, she *had* a motto— An experience in high romance—but Marvin Birch was worried that it might scare off the occasional Texas businessman who was still attached to his cowboy boots and Stetson. As a result, he'd asked her to have an alternate idea just in case.

"Next he'll suggest they put spittoons in the lounge ads," she muttered, combing her fingers through her hair.

Stretching, she grimaced at the stiffness in her shoulder muscles and at the small of her back. There was such a thing as knowing when to quit and this was it for her. Her gut instinct told her that the romance theme would satisfy her client; it complimented the unique style of the hotel's architecture, as well as the mall's. If Birch didn't like it, he could come up with his own idea. She was going to call it a night.

She collected all the paperwork on the account and locked it in her credenza. That still left half a dozen phone messages on her desk and a list of supplies she needed Tess to appropriate tomorrow from their stingy supply custodian. Satisfied that she was leaving things in reasonably good shape, she retrieved her purse, attaché case and shawl and left her office.

At the end of the darkened hallway she could see one of the custodians' cleaning carts parked outside an office like a lonely sentinel. Behind her she heard voices and laughter, indicating she hadn't been the only one to put in extra hours. Cliff Margolis and Pete Harkness, she thought hesitating. She considered backtracking to say good night; but they, too, had an account problem to iron out and she wasn't about to get lured into a trialogue about that, no matter how much she normally enjoyed tossing ideas back and forth with them.

The lateness of the hour prompted only a short wait for an elevator. As she stepped into it, she thought about her day and decided she was lucky to feel as sane as she did.

Between her mother and Birch she'd been pushed to an emotional limit. All she wanted to do now was go home, pour herself a glass of Chablis and have a long soak in the tub enhanced with a decadently expensive bubble bath she saved for just this kind of evening.

Once outside in the street Blair drew a deep breath, grateful to inhale something that wasn't completely recycled or refrigerated. The air was balmy, slightly more humid than usual. She didn't even wrinkle her nose at the faint scent of diesel fumes that lingered after a day's heavy traffic. Tossing her Italian print shawl over her left shoulder, she crossed the street, heading for the parking garage where she kept her car.

This was, she admitted to herself as she hurried to the multitiered building, her only dislike about long working hours. Though it was late spring and, therefore, still light, there were no security guards and too much accessibility for anyone to feel completely safe when they walked alone to their car in the evening. Especially a woman. Luckily she was parked on ground level and within view of the office building.

She dug her keys from her purse, but upon approaching her white Mercedes, she discovered something that would make them all but useless. The rear tire on the driver's side was flat.

"I don't believe this," she cried, stooping down to get a closer look. "If this doesn't top off a thoroughly rotten day..."

The tire was deflated almost to the wheel's rim. She carried a can of that aerosol fix-it goop in her trunk precisely for such an emergency, but she knew she could be carrying an entire case and it wouldn't help. "Damn," she muttered, rising.

Unlocking her door she tossed in her things. Then pushing up her sleeves, she returned to the trunk to get out the spare tire and jack. She might hate messing with this nasty job but, having grown up on a farm, she was used to it.

However, when she had the car jacked up off the ground, she was reminded that sometimes determination and know-how alone weren't enough to get the job done. More than anything a stubborn nut required strength to break it loose.

"Come on," she gasped, putting her whole body into the effort. But she only succeeded in forcing the lug wrench off the nut.

Thoroughly frustrated she stood, eased the wrench back on the nut and raised her foot to kick against the crossbar. The nut gave...but so did the wrench, slipping off and striking her on her shin.

"Ow!"

"Having problems?"

With a gasp Blair spun around—no easy feat when balancing on one foot and rubbing a throbbing leg. She hadn't even heard him coming up behind her, yet there he stood not ten feet away, his hands on his lean hips and a hint of amusement flickering in his dark eyes. Though she couldn't say she was thrilled to see him again, she had to admit he was the preferred choice when considering the alternative could easily have been a mugger.

She shifted her hand to her chest and exhaled in relief. "You scared me half to death."

Michael Bishop offered an apologetic smile that once again transformed his face into something more than she expected. "Sorry." He stepped closer. "Are you hurt?"

"I suppose my pride's suffered the worst damage. What are you doing?" she demanded when, dismissing her reply, he crouched down and inspected her bruised leg himself. The feel of his fingers moving over her sent her heart leaping again.

"Just making sure you didn't break the skin. If you did I was going to get some cream and a Band-Aid from my first aid kit. Legs like these should be taken care of."

Blair inched out of his reach. She didn't want him touching her. The very idea was too intimate, too unsettling.

"Really, I appreciate it, but I'm all right. It's just that this stubborn nut didn't want to come off."

Still crouching, Michael shifted slightly and finished unscrewing it. "I'm impressed at your ingenuity. Most women would either be near tears by now or at least inside calling for a service truck."

"I'm not most women."

He slipped off his glasses and slid them into his pocket. "I've noticed," he said, giving her a sidelong look.

Blair barely heard him; she was too busy thinking about the shiver of response that sped through her. He looked so different without his glasses, so much less *dismissable*. Strange that they'd been alone together in her office on numerous occasions and this was the first time she experienced the feeling that he could be, well, dangerous.

He'd already returned to the task of unscrewing the remaining nuts and, as if rejecting her fanciful thought, Blair shook her head at herself. She'd better start thinking about scheduling her vacation. When she began to think of corporate plant men as dangerous, it was time to admit her hectic job was getting to her.

"It was only that one nut that was giving me problems," she told him as he jerked the flat tire off the hub. "If you're pressed for time, I could finish that."

"I'm in no rush. Besides, there's no sense for both of us to get dirty. Where'd you learn to get so comfortable around cars?"

"I grew up on a farm."

He shot her a look that could only be described as pleased. "No kidding? Me, too. Here in Texas?"

"Mmm. A little beyond Fort Worth near the Brazos River. You?"

"Oklahoma. Those were the good old days."

"If you say so."

If he noticed the bitterness that underscored those dryly spoken words, he gave no indication. He only rolled the flat tire to the back of the Mercedes and hoisted it into the trunk. Returning, he took the spare leaning against the bumper and lifted it onto the bolts.

"There's nothing quite like waking up in the morning to the sounds of roosters crowing and cows mooing—"

"Not if the rooster has his internal clock confused and he starts up at a little past midnight and keeps going until dawn," Blair drawled.

Grinning, Michael rubbed at his cheek with the back of his hand. "You're supposed to leave me with my fond memories. What about after a hay harvest, crawling on top of a pile of those rolled stacks, surveying the world and smelling that rich earth smell?"

"What about going out to feed the pigs before school on a dark February morning and it's raining so hard the yard's one giant mud pen so that you wind up with so much mud on you that you're in worse shape than the pigs?"

Michael gave her a sheepish look. "I used to blackmail my brother into handling those chores."

"Mine was too young."

He was nice, she thought, beginning to relax. She leaned back against the Mercedes and watched his large, nicely shaped hands deftly screw the nuts onto the bolts. Her reaction earlier must have just been her tension over being alone in the garage, along with fatigue. Here was a fellow ex-farmer who understood the rigors of the life and still missed it.

"Is he the one who gave you the amaryllis?"

It took Blair a moment to realize what he was talking about. "Oh, yes." She struggled to think of a way to change the subject, not wanting to compound the lie with even more. "Isn't this a long day for you?"

Having tightened the nuts by hand as much as he could, Michael finished the job with the lug wrench. "Somewhat. One of our clients had a thrip problem."

"I beg your pardon?"

"Thrips. Little sucking buggers that feed off plant juices. They attack amaryllis, too. I think this batch got in with a pot of chrysanthemums. You get a few thrips in an office with a good supply of dracaena and philodendron, before you know it they forget all about missing the great outdoors. They set up housekeeping, have a herd of baby thrips and that's it—you have an epidemic on your hands."

"I see." Blair wasn't sure if he was serious or teasing her and had a difficult time keeping a straight face. "So, did you manage to stave off this potentially catastrophic episode?"

"Oh, sure. Have spray gun, will travel." He replaced the hubcap and tapped it in place with his fist. "Of course, toads would be a more natural insecticide, but I don't think that would have gone over very well with some of the ladies."

As he cranked the car back to the ground and collected the jack and wrench, Blair found herself having second thoughts about him. Maybe Tess's idea that she invite him to escort her to her brother's wedding hadn't been so crazy after all. Maybe it could work. He seemed amiable enough, and he certainly was attractive. His leanness was misleading. While he'd been changing her tire, she'd noticed the broad spread of his shoulders beneath his shirt. Why, put him in a suit and he would indeed look "yummy," as Tess had described.

"Do you always work these long hours?" he asked, returning the equipment to the trunk. "What I mean is, I hope this isn't making you late for a date or anything."

"Oh, no. My days are, admittedly, long and most of the time all I want to do when I get home is hibernate. But I love my work, so I suppose I'd have to say it's worth it."

"I've noticed some of the drawings on your desk. You're good."

"Why—thank you."

He'd noticed. The news filled her with an unusually warm sense of pleasure and, while he slammed the trunk and wiped his hands on the handkerchief he drew from his jeans pocket, she made a quick decision.

"Michael," she began, crossing her arms and peering at him from beneath her lashes. "I have a confession to make. That story this morning about the sick amaryllis wasn't true. The real reason I came looking for you was to ask you to go to my brother's wedding with me on the second Saturday in June. It's a long complicated story and I won't bore you with the details. The crux of my problem is that I have a mother who won't hear of me attending this auspicious occasion alone, and seeing that I'm—well, seeing that there isn't anyone—Oh, heck. I don't have anyone to ask and I thought maybe I would ask you. Only I chickened out in the last minute."

His dark eyes warmed, his smile changed from bemused to tender. He swept his eyes searchingly over her face in a way that made her feel as if he was tempted to do the same thing with his fingers. And then, abruptly, he lowered his head and briskly shoved the handkerchief back into his pocket.

"That's nice, Blair, and I really appreciate the invitation—as well as your honesty. But...I can't. I have a conflicting engagement for that Saturday."

She didn't think she could feel more foolish than she had that morning. She was wrong. Completely humiliated and inexplicably hurt, she had to consciously make an effort to keep the smile on her face.

"Oh. Well, don't worry about it. After all, it was only a brainstorm." She fiddled with her keys and took a step backward. "I'd—um—better be going. Thanks for changing the tire."

"Blair." He hesitated as if struggling over what to say. "I wish things could be different. I would have liked to take you to the wedding. Maybe some other time?"

"Some other time." She reached behind her and felt a fingernail snap as she made contact with the door handle. Her smile felt just as brittle. "Thanks again."

She couldn't get out of there fast enough. As it was, she almost left her pass in the exit meter. Racing through the near empty streets of Dallas, she berated herself for asking him in the first place. "Another engagement"—sure. He'd simply been too polite to say he didn't want to go!

"Damn," she muttered, racing through a yellow light.

Damn, Michael Bishop thought, hitting the steering wheel with his palm as he sat in his driveway. All the way home the scene with Blair had played over and over again in his head, refusing to let go—and it should have.

This wasn't the first time a woman had invited him out. His work brought him in contact with a lot of women, and many weren't shy about taking the initiative these days. Not that it bothered him by any means. He considered himself open-minded enough to accept changing social trends. Yet he always turned down their offers. He had no choice in the matter. However, for the first time since he could remember, he wished he *did* have a choice.

He heard the scratch on the outside of the station wagon and opened the door to find his basset hound sitting there patiently waiting. "Hey, Rocket, old man," he murmured affectionately. "How're things?"

The dog toppled over and offered his bulging belly for rubbing. Michael managed to get out without stepping on him and bent down to give him the attention he wanted.

"Harriet fed you again, didn't she? Don't look away, I can feel it. What was she baking this time that you smelled and couldn't resist? Chocolate chip cookies? Banana nut bread?" Straightening, he nudged the sagging-eared hound with his toe. "All right, pal, let's move it out. And you can forget about sharing pizza with me tonight. From the looks of things, one more bite of anything and you'll explode."

He checked his mailbox and found the usual variety of junk mail and bills; no more than he expected, considering the remaining members of his family and his few friends preferred to phone instead of writing. Usually he preferred it, too. But tonight he found himself thinking that it might be nice to have discovered one letter, even a postcard. Tonight it seemed important to know that someone was thinking of him.

It was Blair Lawrence's fault, he decided, frowning as he retrieved his newspaper, then went through the breezeway separating his house from his garage. She'd knocked him off balance with her invitation. In the six months he'd been working for Lone Star Plantscaping, she'd never deviated from her strictly business attitude—and she was proving to be his one temptation.

As Michael stepped up onto the redwood deck in the back of his house, he considered his small fenced yard. He could just make out the climbing roses blooming profusely against the back stockade fence and the cardinals, mockingbirds and sparrows attacking the raised feeder for an evening snack before calling it a day. Below it the flower beds were lush with spring blooms—pansies were now getting competition from an assortment of perennials, creating a natural quilt of color. He needed to get in there and do some trimming and weeding, but not tonight. His heart wouldn't be in it, and he knew it also wouldn't give him the peace he usually took from gardening.

"Yoo-hoo! Michael!"

At the sound of that singsong voice, he turned to see his next door neighbor hurrying down the steps of her own deck and head for the wisteria-covered trellis that joined their yards. Sighing inwardly—because even though he liked Harriet Hooper he wasn't in the mood to talk—Michael went to meet her.

She was a diminutive woman with a round, dimple-cheeked face that reminded him of a Cabbage Patch doll. She kept her short hair permed and could never be caught without earrings or a bit of rouge and lipstick. Now as she hurried toward him, already dressed for the night in a hot pink, short-sleeved caftan and a matching net cap over her hair, the scent of rosewater she liberally splashed on herself competed with the fragrance drifting over from the flower beds.

"Late night, dear," she said in lieu of a greeting. She shoved a covered dish into his hands. "Here. Put this in your microwave for two minutes on high. It's stuffed cabbage. I left out the rice because I know you don't like it."

Michael shook his head but couldn't quite keep from smiling. He and "Harry" had been neighbors for six years. A widow of a former police officer whose children were all grown and off to various corners of the world with the armed forces, she'd transferred her maternal instincts to him with the relief of a lost homing pigeon spotting a place to nest. When she wasn't trying to turn him into the human version of the Goodyear Blimp, she was killing his dog with kindness.

"Thanks, Harry, but you really shouldn't have. I could have warmed up a pizza."

"Phooey. This is healthier for you and you eat it all, you hear?" she added, playfully punching him in his flat belly.

"Yes, ma'am." A mosquito buzzed around her head and, batting it away, Michael used it as an excuse to escape. "You'd better get inside before these bloodsuckers discover what a soft-skinned woman tastes like."

Harriet tittered like a schoolgirl, but before she ran back inside she drew a chocolate chip cookie from her pocket and tossed it to Rocket. Once she was gone Michael looked down at the sad-eyed dog who continued to hold the cookie between his teeth.

"Had enough, did you? Well, I won't look—go ahead and bury it if you want. But hurry up or I'll leave *your* sugar-saturated carcass to the mosquitoes."

Once the cookie was buried and they were inside the Cape Cod style house, Rocket sprawled on the cool kitchen linoleum while Michael shoved Harriet's stuffed cabbage into the refrigerator and took a frozen pizza out of the freezer. While he waited for his dinner to heat, he opened a beer and sat down at the kitchen table to browse through the paper.

But even before he could do more than scan the headlines, his thoughts returned to Blair and what had happened in the parking garage. How pleased he'd been to hear her invitation. How tempted he'd been to accept. Only training had held him back; only discipline had reminded him that technically he was still an agent for the FBI and, though his current assignment was merely to observe the goings-on in the consulates in Blair's building, he knew he had to follow all the same rules as if this were a highly sensitive case.

It was nothing less than what he'd agreed to when he'd decided he would take this job instead of quitting. Several months ago he'd discovered he'd had enough of the life. Ready to resign, his boss had talked him into taking this cushy job, a way to allow him to continue with the Bureau until he was vested for his pension. But he knew what was really behind the suggestion. His boss also believed that within weeks he would be bored stiff and ready for reassignment.

He was wrong. Michael may once have left home thinking there had to be a better life than the tough, often unappreciated work he'd experienced as a boy, but over the years he'd gained a new perspective. He hadn't been lying to Blair when he'd said he loved the life. Back then, he may not have, but he did now. It had taken him a while but he knew the land was in his blood, and the only "good life" was one that would allow him to work with it.

There was something else, rather some*one* that he wanted, as well. While it had taken him a while to admit it to himself, he faced it now with the same honesty he did his other revelations. He wanted Blair Lawrence. He'd wanted her from the first time he'd seen her six months ago.

She was the kind of woman that stuck out in a crowd. Not because she was tall, though he thought her long legs were a definite asset, but because she was striking. There was a dark sensuality about her, a smoldering something that was held in check by strong willpower. Passion. He found it a lot more interesting than fragile faces and sweet dispositions.

No one could mistakenly call Blair Lawrence sweet. Her opaque brown eyes were too wise, her oval face too defined and her body too voluptuous. She'd given him more than a few sleepless nights over the past several months, and he wanted more.

Strange. Romance had never been a priority in his life. In a way he'd once been something of a love 'em and leave 'em type. It seemed a nasty joke that now that he'd met someone who he wanted to explore this new side of himself with, he was supposed to keep his distance. But there *were* Bureau rules....

Exhaling heavily, he finished off his beer and stood to check on his pizza.

Bureau rules, he fumed again a few hours later as he lay in bed and tossed away the book he was trying to read. They were a pain in the butt.

At first he thought he would have no problem with following the instructions he'd been given not to develop any close relationships with anyone in the building so as not to jeopardize his cover. But he was only kidding himself. Try as he might, he couldn't keep her out of his thoughts, and tonight's invitation had made him realize just how vulnerable his resistance to her really was.

Yet, was he willing to pay the consequences for something he wasn't sure had any future in the first place?

"The hell with it," he muttered, sitting up and swinging his legs over the side of the bed. Then he reached for the phone.

*   *   *

Blair tossed away the magazine she'd been reading in bed and rolled over on her stomach. Her mother was just going to have to understand that she wanted to go to Tim's wedding alone and that was that. Somehow she would make her accept that she wasn't her brother, that as happy as she was for him, their lives went in opposite directions with totally different needs and goals, and Blair's didn't include having a lifelong companion. She'd been self-sufficient for too many years.

Tim had never had to worry if there was going to be food on the table or decent clothes to wear to school. Granted, he'd had his share of chores while growing up, but by the time he'd been old enough for chores, the fence posts were already dug, barbed wire strung and the ground had been softened from several years of tilling. He'd also been spared the degradation that came with being poor—and with the heartache that came from relying on someone irresponsible to support you. She and her mother hadn't, and early on she promised herself that she would never be put in that position again.

She was ambitious and acknowledged it with pride. It had taken her six years to get through college and for most of those years she'd worked full-time waiting on tables, as well as continuing to help her mother on the farm. There had been little time or inclination to think about dating and romance. There still wasn't but it annoyed her when anyone suggested that as a result she was somehow failing as a woman and that she'd better grab someone quick before it was too late.

What could a man give her that she hadn't already achieved for herself? She'd bought herself a nice little condominium near exclusive Turtle Creek. She had a brand-new Mercedes, and for Christmas she'd paid off her mother's mortgage on the farm. As for sex, Blair concluded, it was highly overrated. So who needed a man in their life?

Who needed Michael Bishop?

The phone ringing startled her and she knocked the magazine off the bed as she sat up. She stared at it suspiciously, wondering whether her mother had developed some form of ESP and was calling to add her two cents to her internal pep talk. She almost convinced herself not to answer—but whoever was calling was persistent. Annoyed, she grabbed for the phone.

"Hello!" she snapped into the mouthpiece.

"Blair...this is Michael Bishop. I didn't take you away from anything, did I?"

Did black thoughts count? "Ah—no. I was just—tallying some figures and didn't want to lose my place." *Michael?* What could he possibly want?

"You mean you're still working? I hope your company appreciates your dedication."

"I'm sure they do. What can I do for you, Michael?"

Hearing the slight chill in her voice, Michael hunkered over and, resting his elbows on his knees, stroked his whisker-roughened jaw. "I called to apologize again...and to ask you if the offer's still open?"

Blair didn't know what to say. "I thought you said you had a prior commitment for that date?" she asked cautiously.

"I was able to get out of it. Reschedule actually." That sounded better, he reassured himself. Less like something contrived, although it was.

"You shouldn't have gone to any trouble for me. I wouldn't want you to disappoint anyone."

Else. She'd almost said "anyone else"—he was sure of it, and the realization sent a surge of pleasure through him as if he'd just swallowed some heady wine. Generous with this newfound feeling, he wanted to share it with her. "It was only a ball game, Blair," he said huskily, almost believing himself. "There'll be others. How about it?"

"Well . . ." She would be darned if she was going to be overly grateful. "As I told you, it's only a family wedding. You'll probably be bored to death."

"Are you trying to say you've already asked someone else?"

"Oh, no. But—"

"Then it's settled. I'll let you go now so you can finish up with your work. You can fill me in on the details when I come in Friday. 'Night, Blair." He hung up before she had a chance to say anything else.

There, he thought, stretching out again and gazing up at the ceiling. It was done. He took a deep breath and felt a sense of satisfaction and anticipation.

Could be the old Bard was right, he mused. At times men *were* the masters of their own fate. Only time would tell.

Chapter Three

By Friday Blair assured herself that she had the whole situation in perspective. This was really nothing more than a business engagement not unlike the hotel openings, mall openings and campaign extravaganzas Elliot or one of her other co-workers had attended with her in the past. The only difference was that this time Michael Bishop was filling that need.

But from the moment he walked into her office, all her logic seemed to take a flying leap through the plate glass window.

I don't understand it. There was no reason for her palms to grow moist, she thought, smoothing them over her red skirt just before she stood to greet him; no reason for her stomach to start acting up as if she'd swallowed a mouthful of Mexican jumping beans. He was just a man, she reassured herself, taking in his stone-washed jeans and soft white polo shirt. She often rubbed elbows with chief executive officers and corporate presidents. So what if she was beginning to notice his clothes fit him better than theirs ever would, or for that matter most of the men she knew? Wasn't she an expert at creating an image? Was she going to be taken in by the same type of trim body she used to sell the public on an idea?

"Michael—hello," she began, giving him a polite smile. There, she thought, regaining her composure. This was no different than any other business meeting, casual but still professional.

Michael's smile was warmer by several degrees. "You're wearing my favorite necklace."

The remark immediately threw her off balance and she found herself reaching up to finger the gold choker she wore inside her V-necked white blouse. He paid so much attention to her that he had a favorite necklace?

"Why thank you. Umm—" She gestured to the plastic carrier in which he kept his supplies and gardening tools. "Don't let me keep you from your work. I certainly wouldn't want to throw you off your schedule."

He set the carrier on the coffee table. "No problem. So, are we still on for next month?"

Tess walked into the office, her smile bright with approval and pleasure. Blair had filled her in on things, and ever since she'd been walking around with a silly grin on her face. "Blair, don't forget to ask Michael about the new coffee table plant. Can I get anyone coffee, tea, anything?"

Behind Michael's back Blair waved her hands and shook her head negatively. The last thing she wanted to do was prolong this meeting.

"Nothing for me, thanks," Michael replied.

"*Thank you*, Tess." Blair tilted her head to the door.

As the younger woman left, Michael turned back to Blair and sat down on the edge of her desk. His gaze was admiring as he watched the fluorescent lights reflect off her glossy, sleek hair. "What's this about a new plant?"

"Oh, nothing important." Good grief, she thought, would she ever place the memory of *that* episode behind her? "I've just been having a problem lately with that dieffenbachia getting in people's way, and I thought it might be time to replace it with something else."

Michael pushed his glasses up his nose and considered the plant. He couldn't understand why, but who knew what kind of klutzes stumbled around in her office. "Did you have anything special in mind?"

"Cactus," she said impulsively. It seemed to fit her disposition lately. Dry and prickly.

Nodding Michael glanced around the room. "Maybe several miniature ones in a clay planter. It would compliment the geometric patterns in the upholstery...give it something of a Western flair. I'll see what I can do. Now, about your brother's wedding."

"Blair, have you got time to— Sorry," Cliff Margolis said, pausing two steps into her office and looking from her to Michael, who was stroking the crystal paperweight on her desk. "I didn't know you were with anyone."

Couldn't she even find privacy in her own office? Blair wondered, about to fall back on her dieffenbachia story to explain Michael's presence. She caught herself just in time. What was wrong with her? She didn't owe anyone an explanation. Lifting her chin, she gave Cliff a cool smile.

"That's all right. What can I do for you?"

"I wanted to show you some projected cost runs for a Cadillac commercial I'm developing. You did the one for the dealership in Fort Worth last year and I was wondering if you'd look at my quote and tell me if I'm missing anything." Handing it to her, he gave her a sly wink. "But hey, no rush. Give me a call when you're free."

He was gone before she could think of a suitable reply, and she rubbed the back of her neck, painfully aware that the worst gossip at McGowan and Birch had just gotten the wrong idea about her and the corporate plant man.

"Is this a bad time for you?" Michael asked, watching the smooth, pale skin between her eyebrows pucker. He wanted to stroke away the frown with a caress, or better yet a kiss and settled for briefly touching her hair. "We could do this later."

Sure, by then maybe she could collect the entire secretarial pool in her office, she thought sardonically. Only ingrained discipline kept her from giving in to sarcasm, or moving out of his reach; but as she watched him continue stroking her paperweight, her nerves sent out alarm signals as loud as tornado sirens. Before Michael got the wrong idea about her invitation, she needed to set him straight on a few things. Unfortunately, there wasn't time right now and this definitely wasn't the place.

"Later would be much better," she began, brushing her hair behind one ear. "Is there any way we could meet after work?"

It was more than he'd hoped for. "How about dinner?"

Blair groaned inwardly. Everyone and their barber went out to eat on a Friday night and the thought of running into someone she knew was hardly appealing. "Someplace quiet where we can hear ourselves talk?" she suggested, not quite meeting his eyes.

He smiled, deciding he liked discovering this side of her. For all her assertiveness and professionalism, he was learning that she was really shy around men. It was a rather old-fashioned, charming trait he thoroughly approved of.

"I know the perfect place, if you like Oriental food?"

She nodded, relieved that they at least had that much in common. "What time, and where should I meet you?"

"Meet me? I'll pick you up. I have to learn how to get to your place anyway, don't I?"

She would have preferred meeting him somewhere; however, before she could tell him so, she glanced over his shoulder. The office manager's secretary was out front talking to Tess, but it didn't take twenty-twenty vision to see that she was more interested in what was going on in Blair's office. Enough was enough, Blair decided reaching for one of her business cards. She hastily scrawled her address on the back.

As Michael accepted the card he purposely closed his fingers around hers, prompting Blair to meet his steady gaze. She had gorgeous, dark brown eyes and he didn't want to be cheated of an opportunity to gaze into them, especially since he had to wait so long before the opportunity would arise again.

"Seven okay?"

Blair had to moisten her lips with her tongue because the room had suddenly gone as dry as a desert. "Can we make it eight? Fridays have a tendency to get crazy around here."

"Fine. I look forward to it."

"Listen, Michael, you'll have to excuse me. My boss's secretary just flagged me. I'd better go see what's up."

"I understand," he replied, glancing around, though the secretary had apparently already left. "But Blair?"

Halfway around the desk, she froze like an escaping convict caught in prison searchlights. "Yes?"

"Have a nice day. . . and think about me."

She gave him a weak smile and hurried out of her office. Oh, she would think about him all right, she assured herself as once again she was reduced to seeking refuge in the ladies' room. How was she supposed to avoid it when he was single-handedly turning her plans upside down, and she was feeling as if she'd just jumped off a diving board into a pool of quicksand?

* * *

He was prompt. At precisely eight that evening he was ringing her doorbell. Having arrived home only ten minutes before, Blair decided it was just as well. She didn't need the added burden of dwelling on whether she should change or not, nor did she want time to pace a hole in her ivory living room carpet.

Shutting the refrigerator door on the bottle of Chablis she'd been reaching for, she flattened her hand against the increasingly familiar butterflies nesting in her stomach and hurried to the door. The butterflies grew into condors when she saw that unlike her, he *had* changed, and what a change it was!

Gone were the glasses, the jeans and the jogging shoes. He wore a gray linen sports coat, light gray slacks and a mauve shirt opened at the neck for a casually dressy look. Her mother was going to love him, Blair thought dryly after they exchanged greetings and she stepped back to let him into her home.

"I only arrived a few minutes ago myself," she murmured closing the door behind him.

He shook his head in commiseration. "You work too hard. We're going to have to do something about that."

Blair placed both hands against the lurch in her tummy. "Let me get my purse and I'll be ready to go—unless you'd like a drink?" she asked, belatedly remembering her manners.

"No, thanks. The restaurant has a great plum wine I thought we'd try."

Relieved, Blair excused herself and went to get her purse and slip into her suit jacket. It was really too warm to wear it, but, like armor, it somehow made her feel safer.

In her absence Michael looked around the white-on-white room accented sparingly with a few wildly colored throw pillows and equally dramatic flower arrangements. He whistled silently. The lady had good taste. It only confirmed what he'd surmised over the past six months of covertly observing her: there was a lot of passion in her waiting to be tapped. More than ever he was convinced that he'd made the right decision about bending agency rules.

"Ready?"

He spun around and let his gaze sweep over the striking picture she made in her vivid red suit against the backdrop of white. *More than,* he thought, giving her a nod and a reassuring smile.

"How long have you been with McGowan and Birch?" he asked as she locked her front door and they walked down the geranium lined sidewalk.

"Almost five years. Roger McGowan stole me away from another firm by promising me advancement and a salary commensurate with my abilities. However, little did he know my goals—the standing joke between us is that he's worried about keeping his *own* job."

"Would you like to be a partner in the firm?"

"I don't think so. Partners have to get into the administrative aspects of running a business and I find that—" She was going to say "boring", but then she noticed the vehicle Michael was leading her toward. A pickup? He was taking her to dinner in a pickup truck?

All right, Blair, calm down. After all, this is Texas and anyway, trucks are made to ride as luxuriously as sedans these days.

But getting into one with a narrow skirt was no easy feat. As Michael held the door open for her, Blair did her best to maintain her dignity while climbing up into the cab. It could be worse, she reminded herself as she did an abbreviated snake dance to return the skirt to the vicinity of her knees; he did keep the two-toned blue truck in immaculate condition. Besides, he could have picked her up in that chartreuse station wagon with Lone Star Plantscaping's logo painted on the door.

"I hope you're hungry," Michael said, climbing in on the driver's side and trying hard to keep his eyes from straying to her shapely legs. "This restaurant is family-owned and they really try their best to please their customers."

"You sound like a regular," Blair replied politely. All she really wanted right now was a glass of that wine he'd mentioned. Why was it every time she thought she had her nerves under control around this man, something happened to send them running haywire?

"I pop in there a few times a month." Because he hated to sit at a table alone, he usually ordered take-out. "I suppose in your line of work you get tired of eating out."

Blair shot him a rueful smile. "It's more a matter of getting tired of my bland cooking. Remember, I'm the ex-farm girl, raised on grits, hash and scrambled eggs. As of yet, I haven't had much time to learn to expand on, so any opportunity to avoid my kitchen is grabbed at with relief.''

"My solution is to keep a supply of frozen pizzas in the freezer."

"Shh . . . my thighs only have to hear that word and they dimple."

Michael chuckled, but his answering look was intimate. "I think you like to exaggerate. You look perfect to me."

The ride to the restaurant took only a few minutes, but to Blair, who had to wrestle with an erratic pulse rate again, it felt like forever. When Michael parked the truck, she practically jumped out to avoid his coming around to help her. But there was nothing she could do about the gentle yet proprietary hand he curled around her waist as he met her in front of the truck.

The restaurant was in a plain, white-washed building that wasn't quite part of an older shopping center. Despite the fact that they were so busy Michael had been forced to park in the side alley, Blair wondered what else she was letting herself in for. A moment later when they stepped inside the restaurant, she found herself engulfed in darkness and took an immediate step backward, only to come up against Michael's hard body.

"Something wrong?" he asked, shifting to clasp her waist with both hands.

Without thinking she turned her head to reply and her lips grazed his chin. "I'm sorry!"

"I'm not," he murmured, his voice lowered to a sensuous timbre that, along with his closeness, brought goose bumps to her arms.

"I can't see a thing."

"That's because you're standing in front of another door. They make you go through this dark cubbyhole so that your eyes have a chance to adjust. Once you get inside, everything will seem a lot brighter. Watch."

As he unerringly reached for and pulled the door handle before her, Blair's senses were rewarded with wave after wave of sights, sounds and smells. On every table tiny flames flickered merrily in red glass sconces; from the ceiling hand-painted lanterns were hung to add even more subtle light. Soft flute music drifted out of the shadows and, in the middle of the room, water dripping from a multitiered stone fountain provided a lyrical accompaniment. Enticing aromas from food and flowers coaxed Blair into taking several deep breaths until, feeling her mouth water, she was forced to swallow.

"This is wonderful. I must have been past this place dozens of times. If only I'd known it looked like this inside."

"It just goes to show you that you can't judge a book by its cover," he whispered in her ear, as a smiling hostess came to greet them.

Blair had no time to consider his remark, for upon recognizing a favored patron, Michael was warmly welcomed and he introduced her to Lois Wu, the ageless proprietress. Leading the way through the nearly full restaurant, Mrs. Wu showed them to the corner table she'd been holding for them.

"Will you have a bottle of our plum wine tonight?" she asked as she handed them their menus. When Michael acknowledged they would, she bowed graciously and left them.

Between the delicious smells emanating from the kitchen and reading the menu, Blair realized she was hungry enough not to care about calories tonight. But because everything appealed to her, she had a hard time choosing. The Kowloon duckling with its plum-orange sauce sounded heavenly, but the price on the specialty dish made her shift her glance over to the more standard fare. She didn't know what kind of salary a corporate plant man made, but it couldn't be that great.

Michael leaned across the table. "Your eyes have the look of a little kid staring through the window of a candy store."

"I'm not surprised. I still don't know what to choose."

"How do you feel about duck?"

Was the man a mind reader? she wondered as Mrs. Wu returned and proceeded to pour their wine. "I adore duck, but Michael—"

"She'll have the Kowloon duckling," he said unerringly, "and I'll have the rock cod with cashews. Everything else I'll leave in your capable hands."

Blair waited until the diminutive woman had once again left before eyeing him with gentle rebuke. "Just for that I intend for this to be a Dutch treat."

Midway in lifting his glass, Michael paused. He'd heard of independent women, but this was ridiculous. Dutch treat? What kind of turkeys did she go out with? "My choice of restaurants, my treat."

"But you ordered me the most expensive thing on the menu."

It finally struck him: she was worried about spending his last dollar. Reminded of his role and touched that she could be so sensitive, he smiled contentedly. This was exactly the kind of woman his mother was always dreaming he would bring home. He was tempted to wrap Blair in a giant bow and carry her to Oklahoma this minute.

"A man has the right to splurge once in a while," he murmured with a shrug. Then, touching his glass to hers, he looked deeply into her eyes and added, "But I want you to know it means the world to me that you asked."

Dangerous, Blair warned herself, nearly gulping down her wine; but not in the way she'd originally thought. If she allowed this man to slip any farther past her defenses, he could be lethal. She set down the glass and reached for her purse.

"I think we should talk."

"Me, too. How about if you start with your first memory?"

"I *meant* about the wedding."

"I don't suppose there's anything wrong with going backwards," Michael teased, refilling her glass.

Blair drew out the list she'd made for herself earlier that day and methodically smoothed it out on the linen-covered table. "First of all I want you to know that you needn't worry about bringing a gift. Agreeing to accompany me to the wedding is enough. I'll sign both our names to the card on the gift I bring for them."

"Only if you allow me to pay for half," he drawled.

Too susceptible to his charm, she refocused on her list. "And I think it might be better if we take my Mercedes."

"We can use my truck."

"No! It's a very nice truck," she assured him quickly. "But—I'm going to be wearing a semiformal dress and as we've already discovered, your truck isn't exactly designed for—ah—discreet entrances and exits."

How could he forget? "I'm afraid I can't speak totally from experience—you'll remember I missed out on the exit." When he realized she remained unamused, he did his best to wipe the smile off his face. "Okay, we take the Mercedes. Now, unless you want to talk about what I'm supposed to wear, how about—"

"You look very nice in gray," Blair murmured absently as she frowned down at the list, wondering if she'd left anything off. "By any chance, do you have a more formal suit in that color?"

"Well, yeah, but—"

"Good...and a white shirt, please. I'll leave the tie up to you."

"Gee, thanks." He reached for his wine again and took a bigger gulp, trying to squelch the uneasy feeling that was rising in his gut. Okay, maybe they *did* need to talk about clothes and cars, but did she have to sound so methodical about it? It reminded him of the one time in college he'd had the misguided impulse to be one of the science department's human guinea pigs.

"Now...how do you feel about law?"

About to reach across the table and take Blair's hand in his, Michael stopped. The question confused him. "Compared to what?"

"I meant as an occupation."

"On my list they rank somewhere between politicians and TV evangelists, though I'm sure there are some who—"

"I meant as *your* occupation."

Michael went very still. "Why do I get the feeling that if I ask you to explain that remark, I'm not going to like the answer?"

Oh, dear, Blair thought as a waiter arrived with two cups of corn soup. She wasn't handling this well at all. When the man left them she leaned toward Michael, intent on trying to pacify, as well as explain her position.

"Please don't take this the wrong way, Michael. I think you're a very nice person and I'm glad you've agreed to go with me. But...I'm in this rather odd predicament." Briefly she told him about her dilemma, her mother, Walt and the others who'd already turned her down, and what she thought was a viable solution to her problem. "So, you see, it's not personal. I just want to introduce you as an attorney friend of mine. It would solve all my problems and I'd be eternally grateful."

Michael sat there staring at her and feeling like the world's biggest jerk. She hadn't asked him out because she *liked* him; she hadn't asked him out because she'd been attracted to him, as he'd been to her. She'd needed a body and had decided he would do. He couldn't even take consolation in the knowledge that he had only to whip out his wallet and flash his identification to see his ''worth'' take a pronounced rise. Damn it, it was the principle of the thing!

With a mirthless laugh he slumped back in his seat and shook his head. Boy, when he blew it, he really pulled a beauty.

''May I ask what's so funny?'' she asked stiffly.

''I am. Want in on the joke? I actually thought you liked me. For the last six months I've been driving myself crazy fantasizing about you. Little did I know that the woman I've been putting up on a pedestal is more interested in a man's image and net worth than who he really is.''

Despite feeling the sting of guilt, Blair tried to justify her position. ''I do so care about *who* someone is rather than *what*, but the point is this arrangement wasn't meant as a date in the first place. I told you before I don't have time for that sort of a relationship, and if you got the wrong impression, then, yes, I do owe you an apology. But it was never my intention to insult you. It was only supposed to be a job.''

He was more than insulted, he was hurt, but he was determined not to let her see that. ''Well, you'll understand if I decide to change my mind and pass on your offer for employment, Miss Lawrence. You see, unlike you, I don't give a damn what people see me drive in and I'm not ashamed to let people know what I do to earn an honest living. Now, if you don't mind, I think we'd better get the hell out of here before one of us says something they might really regret."

Standing, he drew out his wallet and, tossing a few bills on the table, gripped Blair's elbow and hurried her toward the exit. A greatly concerned Mrs. Wu caught up with them at the door, but except for a brief though sincere apology, Michael offered no explanation and quickly ushered Blair outside.

Increasing clouds had hurried dusk, but Blair was grateful for that. She was so angry she was near tears. How dare he speak to her as if she'd deceived him. Maybe she *had* been wrong to ask him to be something he wasn't, but she hadn't led him on as he'd suggested!

"Ouch!" She cried out as she stumbled on the uneven pavement in the alley and wrenched her arm free from his grip. "Do you mind? It's a little difficult to walk as fast as you in these shoes."

Because she bent over to rub her ankle, she didn't see the man who emerged from a dark doorway. Because he was too busy glaring at her, Michael didn't spot him, either. Then it was too late. The man was blocking their way and in his hand was a short but dangerous looking knife.

"Okay, folks, let's do this quietly and calmly and nobody'll get hurt."

Blair gasped and would have lost her balance if Michael's reaction hadn't been so quick. One moment he was steadying her and the next she found herself placed safely behind him.

"Easy now. Don't do anything stupid," he told the man.

"Hey—just shut up and hand over your wallet. You, too, lady."

Her heart pounding, Blair immediately began to do as he demanded. However, Michael just shook his head.

"Forget it, pal. Now get lost, or the only ones who are going to score tonight are the cops who'll happily haul your butt to jail."

Blair almost groaned. Hadn't he ever read any of those magazine articles that said you shouldn't threaten a mugger? "Michael..." She gripped the sleeve of his jacket. "Let's do what he says." Dear heaven, the man might not be as tall as Michael, but he outweighed him by at least twenty pounds.

Michael half turned to extricate himself from her hold. "Blair, will you please—"

"Look out!"

Seeing his advantage the mugger had decided to move in on them. Even as Blair cried out, Michael saw him out of the corner of his eye.

With blinding speed he shoved Blair against the side of the building, then swung back toward their assailant, kicking out with his left foot and striking the man in the wrist. As the mugger cried out in pain the knife went flying, landing in the tall weeds growing against the opposite building.

He grabbed his wrist and took off down the alleyway. Michael went after him, but at the end of the alley the man managed to kick over a garbage can, causing Michael to stumble.

Swearing, Michael pushed himself to his feet. Turning the can back upright, he then brushed gravel off his hands. There was no sense in chasing after him now, he thought grimly. The guy had too much of a head start. It was just as well; he didn't need to have a run-in with the police. That would mean showing his ID. Blair would see it and that would be that. Taking some comfort in knowing the man's wrist was probably broken and that he wouldn't be accosting anyone else for a while, Michael smoothed back the hair that had fallen over his forehead and returned to Blair.

She was staring at him as if she'd never seen him before—had been staring like that from the moment she saw his incredible response to the mugger's attack. As he approached she released a pent-up breath and gave him a dazzling smile.

"Where did you learn to do that? You were incredible."

Even though he expected nothing less, for Michael it was as if she was rubbing salt into his wound. With another oath he redirected all his anger and frustration toward Blair.

"Was I?" he said bitterly, closing in on her. "Is that what you're looking for, Mr. Corporate America and James Bond all rolled into one? Well, great. Then you should love this."

Grasping her shoulders he jerked her against him, then closed his mouth over hers for what he intended as a punishing kiss. He had enough anger. It boiled in him. Anger for being played for a fool; anger at letting it happen; anger because deep inside on some level he *wanted* to impress her.

With his lips he forced hers open, with his tongue he staked a claim in a way he suspected that no man had ever dared try before. With his hands he held her a prisoner against his pounding heart, determined that she would never forget the lesson he was teaching her.

Only it all backfired on him.

How could he have known that kissing Blair Lawrence would be unlike kissing any other woman? How could he have known that she would be more potent, more luscious, more than even his fantasies had imagined? How could he have known that instead of fighting him, she would tremble against him and utter such a sexy purring sound that that alone almost made him rigid with need?

The hunger came quickly... one that had nothing to do with his empty stomach. This hunger had to do with his empty soul. He pushed her away before it became irresistible.

For a moment he stared into her dazed eyes that reflected the same incredulous look Blair had given him only moments before. Then forcing her into an abrupt about-face he nudged her toward his truck, pausing only momentarily to carefully pick up the man's knife with his handkerchief and tuck it into his pocket. Later, when he could think straight, he would pass it on to a friend on the police force.

"Shouldn't we call the police?" Blair asked, still trying to get her bearings and figure out what had just happened between them.

"Forget it. He's long gone. Anyway, he won't be bothering anyone else tonight."

They were both subdued during the drive back to her condo. But when Michael pulled up in front of her home and escorted her to her door, Blair took a deep breath, knowing she couldn't let him leave without saying something.

"Michael, I'm sorry. For everything. I realize now that I should have been more honest and up-front about things with you. There's nothing I dislike more in a person than dishonesty and I don't blame you for being angry with me."

He stared down at her, seeing the sincerity shimmering in her beautiful brown eyes and wanting nothing better than to forgive and forget, take her into his arms and drown himself in the heady taste that was hers alone. Start over.

But common sense told him that this was his perfect out. He had been wrong in thinking that he could handle this. She would become more of a distraction than he could have anticipated. He would be kidding himself if he thought he could keep his personal life from interfering with his work—and he couldn't afford that. She was simply the wrong woman in the wrong place at the wrong time and the sooner he accepted that, the better it would be for everyone.

"Maybe we were both wrong," he said flatly.

Blair didn't understand why she was tempted to suggest they try again, but the impulse was strong. However, one look at his closed expression and she knew she would be making a fool of herself if she followed through with the thought.

"Maybe so," she murmured, dropping her gaze. "Well, I guess I'll say good night then."

"Goodbye, Blair."

Michael waited until he heard her deadbolt lock before he returned to his truck. That was that, he told himself. It was a close call but he needn't worry any longer about compromising Bureau rules.

Yet no sigh of relief came as he started his truck and pulled away from her condominium. He took no satisfaction in knowing he'd done the right thing. There was only sadness. The kind that made him feel as though something very precious had shattered in his hands.

Chapter Four

No, Mom, he's not here yet ... Of course, I'm going to be nice to him. But I really wish you would have let me take care of this myself... Yes, I'll call you as soon as I come back from our lunch." After all, what else did she have to do?

A minute later when Blair hung up the phone, she rolled her eyes at Tess and shook her head. "I know she means well, but that woman is going to drive me to drink one of these days."

Grinning, Tess slipped the last letter she'd typed earlier into its folder and closed the file drawer. "You knew this was going to happen the minute you admitted you still didn't have a date."

"Yes, but I didn't think even she could connive someone within twenty-four hours to ask me out to lunch just so I could invite him to a wedding."

"Well, look at it this way, the guy *is* a doctor."

"He's my mother's veterinarian."

"A professional man. Just what you're looking for."

"*I'm* not looking for anyone."

"Excuse me," Tess replied with theatrical intonation. "Of course you're not." She came over to Blair's desk and picked up a signed memo lying on the corner. "You haven't told me what this Dr. Dunkerton is like?"

Blair shrugged. "I've never met him before."

"You mean you didn't even ask your mother to describe him?"

Glancing at her watch she retrieved her purse from her credenza, intent on repairing the lipstick she'd chewed off from nervousness. "Yes, I asked her, but you know my mother—as long as a person doesn't grow hair and fangs during a full moon, he's 'nice looking,' and as long as his picture doesn't hang in a post office, he's a 'good person'."

Tess gave her a worried look. "It doesn't sound good."

No, it didn't sound good, but ready or not Dr. Arthur Dunkerton was coming for lunch in about ten minutes. Martha Lawrence had arranged everything. Blair relined her lips with the poppy-red lipstick that matched her coatdress and sighed into her compact mirror.

It was her own fault. She should never have admitted to her mother that her attempts to find an escort had failed miserably. But after that fiasco last Friday with Michael, Blair had been depressed. It got worse on Monday when he'd come into her office and barely nodded before going on about his business. He'd finished in record time and left without even saying goodbye. In a way, she didn't blame him; he'd probably felt as uncomfortable as she did. But another part of her hurt.

Hadn't that kiss meant anything? It wasn't that she wanted something to come of it; she understood that they were all wrong for each other, that it had been a mistake to ask him to escort her to Tim's wedding in the first place. Still, it *had* happened and now they could never go back to being quite the strangers they had been. Or so she'd thought.

Obviously she'd been wrong; apparently, unlike her, he hadn't been affected. Again and again over the past week, she found herself reliving that moment when he'd pulled her against him and crushed his lips to hers. At first she'd been too stunned to resist and afterward she'd been—what? Mesmerized by the power of him—meltingly so. No one had ever made her feel that much in one kiss and no matter how hard she tried to forget it over the next several days, she hadn't been able to. Yet he'd gone in and out of her office and seemed to have no problem treating her as if she were a total stranger.

She envied him that ability, almost as much as she resented him for it. She'd even imagined a terrific scenario of revenge where Arthur Dunkerton walked in— an Adonis with a stethoscope—while Michael was there to check her plants for infestation and fungus. Too late, Michael would realize his error and—

"Blair? Hello, in there." Tess leaned over her boss's

desk and waved her hand before her face. "Are you all right?"

Blinking, Blair brought her wandering thoughts back under control and nodded. Romantic drivel, she scoffed to herself, as she snapped the compact shut and returned it and the lipstick to her purse. She'd dreamed fairy tales as a child and had believed her father would come back, then later, as an adolescent when she ached for someone to relieve her and her family from their poverty. But she'd grown up and learned that nothing happened unless she did something about it herself.

Michael Bishop kissed well. She needed to accept it and forget it. Her mother had once said that her father had been a great kisser, too, and a lot of good that had done anyone.

"Yes, just a bit tired, that's all," she replied, replacing her purse under her desk. "Would you check with the art department and see if they have those proofs ready for my three o'clock appointment with the S & L people? And on your way, stop by—" Oh, God, she thought as her attention was caught by a movement behind her. She knew it was Friday, but couldn't he have waited to show up until *after* she had left?

Tess gave her a quizzical look before glancing around. "Hi, Michael. Come on in. You aren't disrupting anything." She turned back to Blair. "I know. Stop by Birch's office and see if he'll let you out of the four o'clock staff meeting. You do realize he's going to point out that this is the second time in a week you've asked to be excused?"

She hurried off to run her errands leaving Blair to nervously check her watch again. She reached for the portfolio she'd been reviewing earlier when her mother had called. Silently she prayed that Michael would finish his work and get out before Arthur showed up.

"I'll be out of here in a minute," he said, as if reading her mind.

She glanced up to find him scowling at her and, after giving him what she hoped resembled a careless shrug, returned her concentration to her work. "It doesn't matter. You're not bothering me."

"Fine."

Great, she thought waspishly.

Good for you, he thought grimly. Never mind that he hadn't been able to think straight for a week now. Never mind that every time he closed his eyes, he relived it all again—that moment when he'd let anger and frustration get the best of him and he'd kissed her. And there she sat, not a hair out of place, her red dress making her flawless skin positively radiant. He overspritzed the dieffenbachia and rivulets of water dripped onto the coffee table.

"Please remember that wood stains easily."

He reached for a rag to wipe it away and shot her a sidelong look. "I'm taking care of it."

Blair raised an elegant eyebrow. He needn't get snippy about it. "Where's my cactus?"

Back at the greenhouse, Michael suddenly remembered, but just as quickly he squared his chin. He wasn't about to admit it to her. He'd admitted more than enough the other day.

"We're getting a new shipment of miniatures today and I thought I'd wait to see if there was something that would look good in here."

"Oh." She lowered her gaze and touched her fingers to her necklace, belatedly remembering it was the one he liked. "That's thoughtful of you. Thanks."

He wiped at the table with a vengeance. "Keeping the customer happy just makes good business sense."

Blair understood the underlying message—Don't take it personally. *I didn't do it for you.* Determined she too, could excel at ignoring someone, she went back to her portfolio.

A moment later there was a knock at her door. She looked up to see what her plunging heart told her was her luncheon date. *Oh, Mother,* she thought dismally, *I may never forgive you for this.*

Taking a deep breath, Blair rose to greet her guest. "Dr. Dunkerton, I'm Blair Lawrence," she said circling her desk and extending her hand to the man who broke into a wide grin and strode energetically into her office. "Nice to meet you."

"Call me Art," he replied, sweeping off his straw hat and placing it to his chest as if she were the Statue of Liberty. "I've had the pleasure of knowing your mamma for so long, I almost feel like one of the family." He took Blair's hand and pumped it enthusiastically.

Blair didn't have to look at Michael to know he'd stopped working and was watching them. She could only imagine what he must be thinking and it made it nearly impossible to keep a welcoming smile on her face. "Well, she speaks highly of you, too, Art."

Her mother's veterinarian plopped his hat back on his head, which suited Blair just fine. Without it he looked like one of her uncles. He wasn't an unattractive man—when he kept on the straw cowboy hat. It covered the torturous things he was doing to the six strands of hair remaining on his head. It was simply that he was older than she'd anticipated. She considered the plaid sport jacket he wore over a white shirt and chinos. He reminded her of Cowboy Fred who used to host her favorite Saturday cartoon show—over twenty years ago.

At least she didn't tower over him, she thought groping for something positive. Maybe it was a good thing she'd listened to that inner voice this morning and opted to wear low-heeled shoes.

"Well, let me get my purse and we'll go," she said, collecting the bag and all but hustling him out of her office and toward the elevators. "I hope you like steak," she said punching the Down button. "There's a wonderful place not a block from here that—"

"Sugar, I'm a vegetarian. Working with all those beef critters, you think I could eat one? Why it would be like that Jim Hensen fellow dining on frogs' legs. Get the picture?"

"Adequately."

Blair was racking her brain to think of an alternate suggestion when someone reached around her and pressed the Down button again. Recognizing the silver watch on the masculine arm, she felt a tingling feeling race down her spine. She turned slowly to find Michael directly behind her, his dark eyes glittering with accusation.

"Excuse me, but didn't you mean to go up?" she asked hopefully.

"I need something down in my car."

I'll bet, she thought, watching the speculation in his eyes as he glanced from her to Art and back again. She turned her back on him and when the elevator arrived, the three of them got in and all three reached for the same button.

Art was the only one to find any humor in that. "Think we'll get downstairs any faster?" he chuckled. Blissfully oblivious to the ominous looks Blair and Michael exchanged, he then returned to the topic of food. "How do you feel about pasta? Know of any good Italian restaurants nearby?"

Blair did, but she wasn't about to admit it. She had a long afternoon ahead of her and she didn't intend to endure it with the additional burden of a full stomach. At least at the steak house she could get away with ordering a tiny fillet and a salad.

"Gee, I'm sorry, Art. I don't think I do."

"Mario's."

The suggestion, as well as the sensation of Michael's breath tickling the back of her neck, had Blair stiffening. "I don't believe it's open for lunch," she replied, refusing to turn around.

"It's under new management and they're trying to drum up business."

"Then that settles it," Art said, giving Michael a friendly nod. "Thanks, friend."

"Don't mention it."

"I don't suppose you know if they have any strolling violinists or anything like that? This is our first date and I'm trying to make a good impression on the lady.''

''Lots of luck,'' Michael muttered under his breath so that only Blair could hear.

''Pardon?'' Art asked.

''I said, sorry, but I wouldn't know,'' he replied.

They arrived at the lobby and the doors slid open. Michael brushed against Blair as he reached around her to hold it open. ''Better luck this time,'' he drawled.

''Oh, go mist yourself!'' she muttered.

He told himself to forget about it and *her* and concentrate on his job—correction, jobs. But despite his good intentions. Michael found himself continuously checking the time and getting more frustrated whenever he did.

How could she go out with that guy? he wondered bitterly. He hadn't been fooled into believing there was anything romantic involved, at least not on Blair's part, but if *that* was his replacement she was really scraping the bottom of the barrel. The guy might have been wearing real lizard boots, but his sport coat had been polyester, for heaven's sake, and he'd looked old enough to be her father. A woman like Blair could have any man she wanted. Why him?

What did it matter? The important thing was that he was out of it.

That logic soothed him for less than an hour.

It was nearly two when he found himself heading back to her office. He told himself that it was because of the cactus arrangement. If he'd given up his own lunch time to get it, he might as well deliver it.

When he entered her office she was standing by her drafting table gazing out the window. Daydreaming, he fumed, setting the clay planter down with an annoyed thud.

Startled, Blair swung around. "What are you doing back here?"

"Relax. I'm just making a delivery since you seemed so anxious about this."

She dropped her gaze to the planter and berated herself for the instant of weakness when she'd thought, hoped, he might have come back to talk. "It's lovely. But you didn't have to make an extra trip out here just for me," she said quietly.

"The company doesn't make any money if this stuff sits in the greenhouse."

Her expression turned sardonic. "Of course."

"Is it all right here?" he asked, moving the dieffenbachia onto another table and gesturing to the planter.

"No. Move it over a bit."

"How was lunch?" Michael asked, lifting it and setting it two-thirds of the way across the table.

"Lunch was fine." It had been awful, but she wasn't about to discuss it. No sense in handing the man ammunition with which to shoot her down. Arthur was probably a nice man and a talented vet, but she found it difficult to feign fascination when a discussion centered on delivering breeched calves and examining a goat that's intent on eating your hat. She frowned at where Michael had moved the planter. "I said a little. Not that far over."

Exhaling noisily he picked up the planter and set it in the middle of the table. ''There. Satisfied?''

''Oh, I don't know. Maybe it looked better where you had it before.''

This time instead of picking it up, he merely slid it across the table. Blair gasped and rushed toward him.

''Don't! You'll scratch the finish.''

Michael didn't give a damn about the finish. He wanted to know what had happened at lunch.

Oblivious to his scowl, Blair rubbed at the barely visible mark. ''All I asked was that you move it a few inches over there.''

''Well, why didn't you say so? Let me do it,'' he said reaching for the planter. ''It's heavier than it looks.''

''No, that's all right. I'll do it myself.''

She reached for the planter. A heartbeat later his hands closed over hers. The connection sent a surge of sparks through both and froze them in place.

''Blair—''

''Michael—''

Brown eyes met gray. The air felt hot and fairly crackled with pent-up emotion. Blair felt her knees begin to tremble and the few bites she'd managed at lunch shift precariously in her stomach.

She'd thought him only mildly attractive? As secret emotions sparked silver flames in Michael's eyes and his finely chiseled cheekbones became more pronounced with the tightening of his facial muscles, she knew she'd been nowhere near accurate. He was beautiful and she was fighting a battle with attraction that was hopeless.

"Is he taking you to the wedding?" he asked gruffly.

Knowing she had to end this before she made a complete fool of herself, she dropped her gaze to the large hands imprisoning hers. "Let go, Michael... and go away."

He did... almost. He did let go, and in slow motion, her hands shaking, she returned the planter to the coffee table. But as she made a beeline for the door, Michael came after her.

She saw Tess standing just outside watching them with fascination. Then Michael, faster, slammed the office door shut and locked it.

He grabbed her and swung her around, backing her against it. His long fingers gripped her shoulders, not painfully. but in a way that made her understand she wasn't going anywhere.

"Are you crazy?" she asked. Even her voice shook.

"Undoubtedly. But if I am it's your fault. Satisfied?"

"Me? What are you talking about?"

"I thought I could let you go through with this but I can't. Damn it, Blair, I don't know what you see in that polyester cowboy, but he's too old for you."

"Now see here..."

"No, you see. I'll admit at first I was pretty angry at the idea that you would use me to make an impression on your relatives, but I've come to the conclusion that I don't care what the reason was."

"Blair?" Tess knocked on the other side of the door. "Blair are you all right?"

"She's just fine, Tess," Michael replied. "Now go away." When Blair began to speak, he touched his fingers to her lips. "Answer me. Did you invite him to the wedding?"

This was the man who she'd classified as polite and *safe*? Blair stared at him. In his eyes was fearless determination and passion that made her feel dizzy and weak. The hands that gripped her shoulders possessed incredible strength as well as an indescribable sensitivity. He wouldn't hurt her, but she felt imprisoned in ways she didn't even want to think about.

"No," she whispered. "I couldn't."

"Why not?"

Why did he need to ask her that when she could see he knew the answer himself? She lowered her eyes and concentrated on the dark hairs in the open neckline of his blue shirt.

"Michael, there's no future in this. You know I'm attracted to you, but I don't want to be. It just wouldn't work out and it has nothing to do with you or your job. It has to do with me and who I am."

"Why are you complicating things?" he murmured, a small smile beginning to light his eyes. "I thought this was about a date for a wedding?" He shifted one hand to stroke his thumb along her jawline.

Even as she found herself leaning into his touch, she tried to rationalize. "I'm not trying to complicate it, you are. Don't tempt me, Michael. I don't want to disappoint you."

"Ask me once more," he said his dark gaze wandering over her features as if he were a sculptor about to immortalize her in marble. "Let me take you to the wedding."

Say no, her mind shouted at her. *It won't work. He'll break your heart or you'll break his. You don't have time for this!*

But more than anything she wanted to feel his mouth again.

"Yes," she managed, her throat desperately dry. "Please."

He lowered his forehead to hers and closed his eyes in relief. "Thank you."

"Don't mention it."

"Maybe now I can concentrate on my work."

"Me, too."

He lifted his head a fraction to gaze into her eyes. Then he broke into a wide grin. But just as quickly the grin became a look of smoldering desire. "I know what I promised but, Blair, I've got to kiss you before I open this door again. Just one kiss?"

"Maybe you'd better not ask," she whispered. "It only reminds me that I should say no."

"Good idea," he murmured, sliding his hands up to frame her face and tilt it upward in order to receive the warm pressure of his lips. But as he began to lower his head, he heard a thump. Then another one.

He shifted to peer over to the left—and burst into laughter.

Apparently Tess had really been concerned for Blair's safety because she and another man—he recognised the man's profile as belonging to Marvin

Birch—had their faces plastered against the glass wall in an attempt to see what was going on.

"Take a peek," he told Blair. "They look like flounders."

Blair did and groaned. "How am I going to explain this?"

"Don't," Michael replied with a shrug. With no small reluctance he released her and gave her a crooked smile. "I suppose I'd better get out of here."

"Good idea."

"You'll keep in touch?"

"Yes, but I wonder if you realize what you're letting yourself in for?"

As smoothly as before he stepped closer, until she was once again backed against the door. "Never doubt it," he murmured, his gaze locked with hers. But instead of kissing her as he knew she expected, he unlocked the door and with a wink left her.

Blair lifted her hand to her stomach, vaguely noting that it was getting to be a habit whenever he was in the vicinity. Moments later Tess came into her office. However, rather than giving her the third degree as she'd expected, she announced that Blair had a phone call. Funny, Blair thought, they'd never even heard it ring.

"It's your mother," Tess said, eyeing her bemusedly. "Do you want me to tell her that you're in a meeting?"

Blair shook her head and went to take the call. There was no sense in putting off the announcement of this latest turn of events.

"Hello, Mom... Yes, I guess I did forget to call you back... Yes, you could say it's all taken care of... Art? No, not Art. Michael... No, I know you know nothing about Michael. Want to hear something really funny? I barely do, either."

Chapter Five

"Well, how do I look?"

With one hand on her hip and another stroking her chin, Harriet Hooper circled her neighbor, doing a slow inspection of the tall man in the gray suit. Finally she stopped before him and gave him a toothy grin.

"She'll be so impressed, she'll faint. If she doesn't, send her over and I'll straighten her out."

Laughing, Michael hugged her. "Thanks and I appreciate you taking Rocket for the day. If I knew what time I'd be home, I wouldn't mind leaving him on his own, but—"

"It's my pleasure," Harriet insisted, with a wave of her hand. "I'm going to fill the grandkids' wading pool for him and I've rented one of those Benji movies for us to watch this evening." She reached into the pocket of her orange housedress, drew out a cookie, and tossed it to the mournful-looking dog. "We're going to have a good time, aren't we, sweetie?"

Rocket caught the chocolate chip cookie between his teeth and, after giving Michael a long look, dutifully ate it. The message wasn't lost on Michael, but in an attempt to keep his lips from twitching, he averted his gaze and concentrated on adjusting his tie.

"Harry—umm—try to remember that the vet said he could afford to lose a few pounds, okay?"

"It's only one cookie, dear." She shooed his hands away and straightened the knot herself. "What I want to know is have you told your girlfriend who you really are yet?"

It was just like her to put the entire freight train ahead of the engine, Michael thought wryly. Harry had known of his true profession for most of the six years they'd been neighbors. She said the experience of being a cop's wife had made her more observant than the average person and it had been *she* who'd confronted Michael one day while presenting him with a double-fudge cake, asking him what branch of law enforcement he was in. In many ways he was grateful she knew. She could be trusted to keep his secrets and she didn't mind getting a phone call in the middle of the night, when he had to go out and needed her to use her key to let herself in and take care of Rocket.

But though he'd mentioned Blair to her, he wasn't yet ready to discuss the status of their relationship. Instead he teased her. "Don't you think that label works better for teenagers?"

"You want to argue semantics?"

Ignoring that, he glanced out the back window at his garden. "Are you sure I shouldn't bring her a corsage?"

Harriet scowled at him from beneath her shaved and penciled eyebrows. "If she's part of the wedding party, she'll already have flowers. Even if she doesn't, you don't know what color she's wearing, so how can you bring her a corsage? *And*, Mr. Wiseguy, if you don't want to answer me, say so, but stop pretending that one of us is deaf."

"I'm sorry," he murmured, leaning forward to kiss her on the forehead. "No. I haven't told her about me yet—especially since we haven't been out since that first disastrous dinner. I've asked her and she's always had a conflicting engagement or she's working late."

"She's playing hard to get."

"She's a cautious lady. It might not be a bad idea."

"It's a good thing most of the world doesn't agree with you or else we'd be on the endangered species list. Well, what are you going to do when you two decide you like each other and she finds out you're not who she thinks you are?"

"She's not an unreasonable woman. I think given time to think about it, she would understand why I've had to keep certain things from her."

"The word is *lie*, sweetie, and for your information the woman hasn't been born who thinks rationally when she realizes she's been duped." Harriet shook her finger at him. "Be warned."

Michael held his hands up in surrender. "Hey! Give me a break, I'm only going to a wedding. This is supposed to be a happy occasion."

But as he crossed over Central Expressway and wove through the tree-lined streets of Highland Park toward Blair's Turtle Creek neighborhood, Harriet's words came back to haunt him. She was right in that he was playing a dangerous game. Hadn't Blair told him herself that she disliked deceit? But just as she hadn't intentionally meant to lead him on about why she'd asked him out, he wasn't keeping his background from her because it was something he wanted to do. Mitigating circumstances made it necessary. Besides, since she still seemed determined to keep him at arm's length, why shouldn't he wait before confiding in her?

Yet minutes later when she opened her door to him, he knew she could protest all she wanted; he was determined to see that their relationship would not begin and end here.

"You look lovely," he murmured, his gaze sweeping over her, not once but twice.

Her answering smile was more tentative than he would have liked but definitely warmer than last time. "Thank you."

Her two-piece suit was a pastel pink, the ottoman jacket enhanced by black embroidery on the shoulders. It accentuated her narrow waist as flatteringly as the slim skirt complimented her long legs. It would be much safer, he decided, if he kept his gaze well above the embroidery; but even as he considered her petal pink lips, he found himself selfishly wishing they weren't going to her brother's wedding but someplace else where they could be alone.

"I'm early," he added, conscious that his voice sounded raspy even to his own ears. "I hope it's not a problem?"

It would give them time to get comfortable around each other, Blair thought, stepping aside to let him enter, though it was obvious that she had more of a problem with that than he did. She shook her head. "No. None at all . . . and you look very nice, too."

"Thanks."

Impossibly good. Capable. Sexy. As she shut the door, she briefly touched the back of her hand to her forehead, aware of the sudden feverishness of her skin.

"I thought you might like to get there early to help out or do whatever the sister of the groom usually does."

This time Blair's smile was more natural. "In this case she does her best to stay out of the way of the mother of the groom."

Michael slid his hands into his pants pockets. "I really do have to meet this woman. You make her sound like quite a character."

"As long as that's what you're expecting, you won't be disappointed," Blair countered dryly. She gestured behind her. "Give me a minute to turn on my answering machine and get Tim and Alicia's gift and I'll be right with you. Oh . . ." She was halfway to the phone when she turned around, remembering what else she'd wanted to say to him. "I was thinking . . . why don't we take your truck after all?"

Michael felt his heart expand in his chest. Short of telling him she'd slept as fitfully as he had last night because she, too, had been looking forward to today, he couldn't think of anything that could please him more. "We'll take the Mercedes—I think that dress deserves going in style."

"Then I insist you drive."

Michael decided it was a good thing that she chose that moment to disappear down the hallway because had she stayed, he would have been tempted to abandon all his advice to himself to take things slowly. Her attempt to make him feel comfortable was more than touching. It was going to be a great day, he assured himself, taking a deep breath and sending up a quick prayer of thanks.

Moments later she reminded him not to allow his relief to overshadow his attention to detail.

They'd just gotten into the Mercedes and he'd turned on the ignition. Blair grabbed his arm before he could shift into drive.

"Wait! You've forgotten your glasses."

"I don't need them."

"You wear them at work all the time."

She hadn't said anything the other night, he thought glumly. He decided to approach the situation from the point of vanity. "I hate them, and they really are only a weak prescription."

"Don't be stubborn. Suppose you're stopped by the police? Anyway, you look wonderful in them."

"Yeah? Define wonderful."

"Michael, go get your glasses out of the truck."

He supposed he could live with wonderful. With a parting smile, he went for the glasses.

"But I'm putting you on notice now," he said when he returned. "I'm taking them off as soon as I get there."

They both seemed to relax after that. Once they were on their way and Blair had given him directions for a route that would allow them to skip most of the Fort Worth traffic, they had no problem finding things to talk about.

"So what did we get the happy couple?" he asked.

"A pasta machine, and black satin sheets for their new water bed."

He kept his eyes on the traffic before him but raised his eyebrows. "That's a... unique combination."

"Well, from what I hear, Alicia is a terrific everything-from-scratch cook, so the pasta-maker is primarily for her. The satin sheets are something of a joke between my brother and I. He's wanted a set forever, but since my mother's always done his laundry, he's never had the nerve to get them."

Michael wondered if Blair had ever slept on satin, and then decided he didn't want to know. She would look good, too good to think about her there alone—and he definitely didn't want to think about her being with anyone else.

"Do you two share a lot of confidences?"

"Not really. Almost never before he was in college. There's seven years between us," she explained. "And a lifetime of experiences. I used to envy him for being the younger one."

"You thought your folks were easier on him?"

"My mother." The correction was made matter-of-factly. "My father left us when I was ten."

She said it in a way that suggested it should explain everything. It didn't, but Michael filed the information away, suspecting it was an integral piece in the puzzle to understanding her.

"It must have been tough on you."

"It was tough on all of us," Blair replied, reluctantly remembering in particular those first days afterward. "My mother pulled us through it, even though I know she was crushed...to this day I can tell when she's thinking of him. But a few days after he left, she loaded the shotgun with rock salt and set it by the front door. All she said was that some people were as worthless as a Sunday suit in the Sahara and it was time she accepted that."

Michael's glance held amusement and compassion. "Do you think she would have used it on him?"

"Without a moment's hesitation. Only afterward," Blair added dryly, "she'd probably pluck the salt out of his backside, then feed him a bowl of her cure-all vegetable soup." On the other hand, Blair herself would have been more inclined to finish chasing him off with the butt end of the shotgun. But then she had never quite gotten over the hurt she'd felt over his never even saying goodbye. She sighed inwardly. She hadn't liked herself very much back then, but she couldn't deny that her negative feelings had tensiled her spirit, given her the strength she needed to endure the long haul and make something of herself.

"What's the little smile for?"

Blair gave him a sheepish look. He was really too observant for his own good. ''Remember we spoke of growing up on a farm and I sounded—less than enthusiastic? I was just thinking that maybe it wasn't quite that bad.''

''Uh-oh. If this is confession time, I suppose I'd better tell you that I didn't always love it as much as I said I did.''

''I knew you had to be more human than you'd admitted.''

He chuckled softly. ''I liked it well enough, but I thought there had to be something better, more exciting.''

That wasn't unlike what her father had said to her mother, Blair thought, shifting her gaze to look out the passenger window. ''Did you find it?''

In the beginning he thought he had. There had been opportunity for travel with the Bureau and enough excitement to make those long hours of tedious paperwork and pavement pounding seem worthwhile. Then a year ago when a close friend was killed in an arrest attempt that had gone sour, he'd begun to have doubts—about himself, the system, everything.

''For a while,'' he said quietly.

Blair glanced over at him, saw the sadness shadow his face and wondered what story lay behind it. Normally she gave people the same wide berth she expected them to give her when it came to talking about personal things, but it wasn't that easy with Michael. Those dark eyes could appeal to you as easily as they evaded, letting you see what was going on inside.

"Do you get to see your family much?" she asked, wanting to fill the silence that stretched between them.

"Not as much as my mother would like, but I try to call her every week. I like to use my weekends to go out to my place in east Texas."

"You have a home out there? Where abouts?"

"West of Tyler, and it's mostly woods at the moment, but someday I want to turn it into a wholesale nursery."

She did a double take at that one. Those were big ambitions coming from a man she'd previously believed might be cut from the same cloth as her father. "You *have* taken to this plantscaping business, haven't you?"

"I've learned that I like to see things grow. But so do you."

Blair's laugh was laced with chagrin. "African violets have been known to cringe when I pause to admire them at the grocery store."

"I didn't mean plants necessarily. It can be ideas. You take concepts and build on them until an image has grown out of it that sells a client's product or service and the fruit of your labor isn't only the client's success in business, but often the spawning of something."

Blair gave him a slightly startled look. He actually understood. "I've been trying to explain that to my mother for years. She thinks I'm part of the problem why product costs keep increasing, and she keeps nagging me to go into something useful, like accounting."

"I thought she was after you to settle down and have babies?"

"*That* goes without saying. I keep having this urge to apologize to you in advance for whatever she might say to you today. The last thing I want is for you to feel uncomfortable."

"Hey." Michael reached over and gently squeezed her hand. It felt unusually cool beneath his. "I *do* have a mother of my own, you know. Stop worrying. Whatever happens, I can handle it."

He was right. She needn't have worried about him—at least not in the way she'd thought she might. By the time Tim and Alicia were man and wife, and everyone had moved from the church to the Lawrence farm, Michael had utterly captivated her mother and was well on his way to charming everyone else, as well.

"I like him," Martha Lawrence whispered to her daughter as the last guest passed through the reception line and the two of them headed for the kitchen. "You make sure you don't chase him off."

"Of course not, Mom. In fact I was considering hog-tying him to my dinette table. As hard as it is to find a good man these days, there's no sense in taking any chances."

Her mother tossed off her dry humor with the same ease she did her flower-adorned straw hat. "Don't forget you're not going to stay young forever."

"If I do, I'm counting on you to hang around and remind me." Blair watched her mother slip an apron over her yellow polka-dot dress, then take two large pitchers of iced tea out of the refrigerator. "Mother, what are you doing? I thought the caterer was going to take care of all that?''

The small, wiry woman passed one to Blair and nudged her toward the door. ''You have no idea what they wanted to charge for a couple gallons of water and tea bags. Anyway, the kids like the way I sweeten mine and you know your Aunt Violet won't touch the champagne.''

''Well, as long as it's only the tea...''

''I have some deviled eggs in the fridge, too, so keep an eye on the tables and if the platters begin to look empty—oh, Lord, will you look at that swan. We'd better tell the photographer to get a picture or two of it before it's nothing but a pan of water. I don't know why Alicia didn't want the one made out of guacamole. At least we could have eaten it.''

''I think it looks lovely,'' Blair said, setting her pitcher on one of the tables. She reached for a glass of champagne only to have her hand swatted by her mother. ''Not yet. I need you to help me carry out the chips and pretzels.''

''Mother, we don't need chips and pretzels. Look at all this food.''

''The kids don't want that stuff. You watch. Within fifteen minutes they're going to be emptying their plates into my planters. Come on.''

''But Michael—''

''Is doing fine. Look over there. He's got your Great Aunt Virgilenne smiling. That old sourpuss hasn't smiled since Stevenson lost the presidential bid in '56.''

SILHOUETTE DELIVERS FIRST-CLASS ROMANCE— DIRECT TO YOUR DOOR

Mail the Heart sticker on the postpaid order card today and you'll receive:

— 4 new Silhouette Romance™ novels—FREE
— a lovely gold-plated chain—FREE
— and a surprise mystery bonus—FREE

But that's not all. You'll also get:

FREE HOME DELIVERY

When you subscribe to Silhouette Romance™, the excitement, romance and faraway adventures of these novels can be yours for previewing in the convenience of your own home. Every month we'll deliver 6 new books right to your door. If you decide to keep them, they'll be yours for only $2.25* each and there is no extra charge for postage and handling! There is no obligation to buy—you can cancel at any time simply by writing "cancel" on your statement or by returning a shipment of books to us at our cost.

Free Monthly Newsletter

It's the indispensable insider's look at our most popular writers and their upcoming novels. Now you can have a behind-the-scenes look at the fascinating world of Silhouette! It's an added bonus you'll look forward to every month!

Special Extras—FREE

Because our home subscribers are our most valued readers, we'll be sending you additional free gifts from time to time in your monthly book shipments, as a token of our appreciation.

OPEN YOUR MAILBOX TO A WORLD OF LOVE AND ROMANCE EACH MONTH. JUST COMPLETE, DETACH AND MAIL YOUR FREE OFFER CARD TODAY!

*Terms and prices subject to change without notice. Sales tax applicable in NY and Iowa.
© 1990 HARLEQUIN ENTERPRISES LTD.

Sure enough, Blair saw that Michael was hunched down beside the old woman in the cane rocker and whatever he was saying to her, he had her giggling and covering her mouth with a lace-gloved hand. Shaking her head Blair followed her mother back into the house.

It was a full fifteen minutes later—after warning her mother that the canopy-covered tables would collapse if they added anything else—that she went in search of her date. The band was playing a Texas two-step and Tim and Alicia were in the center of the patio leading off the dancing, not only looking blissfully happy, but completely oblivious to everyone and everything going on around them.

"Looking for me, I hope?"

Blair swung around to find Michael jerking backward to keep from spilling champagne from the two glasses he was holding. "As a matter of fact, yes. I hope one of those is for me—or has my family already driven you to becoming a two-fisted drinker?"

"You're too hard on them," he said, handing her one of the glasses of chilled wine. "They're no different than anyone else's family."

As she took a long sip Blair glanced around, taking in children playing hide-and-seek beneath linen-covered tables, women cloistered around the buffet—no doubt discussing the attributes and deficits of the offered fare—men slipping out of suit coats and ties and switching from champagne to beer, and the younger set moving to the band's lively music.

"After I've had about three more of these, I might reconsider. But remember, I've known them longer than you have." She turned back to Michael, finally noticing that he hadn't yet removed his jacket or tie, yet looked comfortable despite the rising temperature. "You know you needn't try to make *too* good of an impression. You can take off that jacket if you'd like."

"You're not dressed for this heat any more than I am and I don't see you slipping out of anything."

"But I'm not wearing as much underneath this jacket as you are."

Michael lifted his glass to his forehead. "I think the temperature just rose five degrees."

Blair tried to give him a reproachful look but failed. "And to think I used to believe you were shy."

Gently grasping her elbow he drew her under the protection of the canopy. "Why don't you tell me what else you've been thinking about me."

"Michael . . ." Blair downed the rest of her champagne, knowing she would need much more if he was going to start using that low, sexy voice on her. "Don't flirt with me. Not today."

"Feeling vulnerable?" he asked, reaching for a bottle of champagne and refilling both their glasses.

"Weddings have a tendency to do that, even to die-hards like me."

"You're not a diehard, you just haven't met the right man yet. I like your brother. Of course, it helps that he thinks you're something close to terrific. Do you know he gave me his blessings to pursue you—after I assured him that my intentions were honorable, of course."

"My brother indulged in his share of libations at his bachelor party last night. He's not to be taken seriously until he's been back on coffee for a week."

Michael touched his glass to hers and smiled deeply into her eyes. "Okay, fight me if you want to, but I should warn you that I intend to charm your entire family until they force you to accept that I'm not going to be chased off."

"Why?" she asked, tilting her head to gaze at him with simple curiosity. "Why me? Why now?"

It wasn't a question he could easily answer without telling her more about himself then he dared. "I told you before, I've been attracted to you since the moment I saw you."

"It's amazing that you've resisted me as long as you did."

"You think because I haven't asked you out the feelings weren't there?" His shrug was deceptively casual. "I know what you'd say if I asked. But that didn't keep me from looking at you and liking what I saw."

Still sensitive about her earlier behavior toward him, Blair lowered her gaze to her glass. "I wish I could wipe that episode out of my memory. More important I wish I could wipe it out of yours."

"You know what I remember more? The glass of punch you brought me when I came in to check on the plants during your office Christmas party. It was my second time in your office and you were wearing a green knit dress with a sequined poinsettia on the right shoulder. It was one of the few times I saw you smile with your eyes and I thought you were the most beautiful woman I'd ever seen."

Blair stared at him not knowing what to say. Yes, she'd been smiling, even giggling. Three glasses of spiked punch on a near empty stomach would do that even to Scrooge, which also explained why she'd brought him the punch. But the sad thing was that she hadn't remembered the event until he'd mentioned it.

"You don't beat around the bush, do you?" she asked quietly, not lifting her eyes above his red paisley tie. "Just drag out the big guns and knock a lady off her feet without giving her any chance to get on her armor."

Michael reached out and gently lifted her chin, forcing her to meet his probing gaze. "You don't need any armor around me, Blair."

He was going to kiss her. She could see it in his eyes and felt it as he lowered them to her lips. He was going to kiss her in front of all these people who'd known her since she was a leggy, scratched-knee kid wearing her ponytail and baseball cap—longer...and she didn't care. She wanted it to happen, probably as desperately as Cinderella had wanted that glass slipper to fit.

But even as she began to lower her lashes to receive his kiss, she felt a small but determined force thrust against her legs. With a bemused frown she glanced down to see a blond mop of hair and red and white layers of eyelet cotton.

"Samantha Lynn...what are you doing?"

"Uncle Mike gonna dance me," the child replied, wrapping her chubby arms around his legs and gazing up at him with blue eyes that challenged the sky's brightness.

Though he was laughing as he picked her up, there was frustration in Michael's gaze as he looked back at Blair. "Angel face, you have lousy timing, do you know that?"

"You pwomised, Uncle Mike."

"Yeah. You pwomised, Uncle Mike," Blair mimicked, while he put down his glass to keep hold of the squirming bundle in his arms. The answering look he gave her had her tingling all over and she wrapped her free hand around her waist.

"Have two more glasses of that stuff and we'll pick up where we left off when I come back," he told her.

"Oh, no. I'm about to switch to my mother's iced tea, even if it does have enough sugar in it to rot out every tooth here."

"Uncle Mike hur-wee. They play'n the Cotton-Eyed Joe!"

"Bye," Blair sang, wiggling her fingers in farewell.

But her escape was only temporary. Less than two hours later someone lifted Alicia onto a cleared off table and the band's lead singer told all the single women to gather before her. Blair's mother gave a whoop of delight and, grabbing her daughter's hand, pulled her to the forefront of the group.

"Mom!" Blair tried to disengage herself without creating a scene. "I'd rather not do this. Let me go sit with Aunt Violet for few moments. I haven't had a chance to do more than any hello to her all day."

"Nice try, but you're staying here," Martha Lawrence said, centering her daughter in line with Alicia's bouquet with the precision of a pool player about to make a difficult shot. Then she waved to her son's new wife. "Alicia, dear! Here she is."

"*Mother,*" Blair ground out between clenched teeth. She folded her arms across her chest. "That does it. I refuse to catch that—"

Before she could finish Alicia flung the bouquet over her head. Arms, seeming to belong to Blair—except for the yellow polka-dot sleeves—reached up and grabbed it, then crushed it against Blair's chest.

"She caught it!" Martha Lawrence shouted gleefully while forcibly wrestling one of her daughter's hands free and wrapping it around the bouquet. "My baby caught it!"

"You're impossible," Blair muttered, accepting the flowers only because she didn't want to damage them.

"Bachelors! Bachelors!" The cry rose around them. "Line up!"

Blair wasn't consciously aware she was looking for Michael in the crowd, until their eyes met across the yard. He glanced down at the bouquet in her hands and broke into a mischievous grin.

"Oh, you wouldn't," Blair groaned, though Michael was too far away for him to hear her.

But as if he could hear, he loped over to join the group converging before the groom.

"I'm not hanging around to see this," Blair said, beginning to turn away.

Her mother locked her bony but strong fingers around her wrist. "Honey lamb, you know what your problem is? You don't know how to have fun. Relax. It's only a piece of satin and lace.''

"It's where that satin and lace *goes* that's the problem," Blair replied. Not to mention who was going to put it there, she thought, seeing Arthur Dunkerton step up beside Michael.

She was determined not to watch. It didn't matter; as soon as she heard everyone cheering she knew her fate. But it didn't stop her from turning on her heel to try one last attempt at escape. Only her mother, knowing her all too well, stood directly behind her. The gleam in her eyes wasn't unlike the one Blair remembered she wore when she went to the henhouse to choose a chicken for dinner.

"It won't hurt a bit," Michael whispered in her ear.

She gave a start, unaware he had sneaked behind her. Giving him a skeptical look, she allowed herself to be led to the chair someone had set in the middle of the patio.

As she sat down she kept her gaze on Michael, because she knew if she looked at all the other people circling them, she wouldn't be able to go through with the ritual. Though he was smiling at the suggestions and encouragements tossed his way, Michael's eyes were sympathetic as he knelt before her.

"I know you'd rather be trekking up Mt. Everest than doing this," he said low enough so that only she could hear. "But the photographer wants his pictures."

"Uh-huh. And you're just trying to keep everyone happy, right?"

"There's a lot to be said for ceremonies," he replied, trailing his fingers down the back of her calf before closing them around her ankle. "They give us traditions to hand down from one generation to the next."

Although she didn't take her eyes from his, Blair felt everything; the smooth texture of the hand-warmed garter sliding over her foot and up her ankle, his hands—gentle, as tender as the look warming his eyes. "Next you'll be telling me that this will be one of the quaint stories I'll want to pass on to my grandchildren."

"Unless I tell them first."

"Moving a bit fast, aren't you?"

"Merely voicing an opinion based on intuition."

He had the garter up to her knee. As the crowd cheered "More!" Michael purposely looked from the discreet hemline to Blair.

There was something faintly challenging in his eyes. Never one to back away from a challenge, she slightly lifted her skirt to allow him to slide the garter beneath...an inch...two. She felt every centimeter and knew he did, as well. He telegraphed it through his eyes and it sent her pulse racing, heated her from the inside out in a way that the sun never would. She could feel the heat collect in her stomach and rise to her breasts, and when she felt his thumb caress the inside of her thigh, her breath caught at the erotic feeling. As her eyes met his, a muscle twitched in his cheek.

"Michael," she whispered, gripping his wrists.

In reply he slowly inched his hands from beneath her skirt. Then he took hers, lifting them to his lips for a brief kiss that earned him cheers from the crowd. He gently drew her to her feet. "I'll take it off later," he whispered against her ear.

The promise echoed in Blair's ears for the rest of the afternoon, leaving her feeling alternately excited and nervous. A part of her wanted to explore these new feelings with him. She liked Michael and felt an attraction toward him that was profound as well as magical. But another part of her mind was firmly planted in logic. She no longer thought of him as "boring" or a "drifter"; however, that didn't mean she was ready for a serious relationship. Yet throughout the afternoon, whenever she found him near, that resolution had a tendency to seem more than a little vague.

After Tim and Alicia were sent off in a shower of rice, people began to leave. Others determinedly returned to their celebrating. Michael asked Blair to show him around the farm and when they ended back at the rose-covered archway leading to the yard, he tugged at her hand to detain her a while longer.

"I think the lady who thoughtfully returned the bride's bouquet so she could have it preserved deserves a flower of her own," he said, breaking off one of the velvety red blossoms and tucking it into Blair's hair.

She couldn't repress a smile. "Have you always known the right thing to say and do?"

"If I seem that way, it's only because I feel comfortable around you," he replied, caressing her cheek with the back of his fingers. "For instance, I know you're feeling a lot of complex things right now and that you'd like me to take the burden of decision making off your shoulders.''

Here we go again, she thought, drawing a deep breath. "You think so?"

"Positive," he whispered, lowering his head. "I'll prove it to you."

His lips brushed against hers with the lightness of a breeze. Then he deepened the pressure slightly, coaxing her to accept the slow invasion of his tongue. As it moved over hers on a journey of exploration as much as seduction, he framed her face within his hands.

Blair felt cherished and a soft sound of approval rose to her throat. The potent fragrance from the roses added to the heady feeling, or was it simply Michael's magical power over her? As a bee buzzed around her head, joining with the buzzing going on inside her, she rested her hands against his chest and drew back for a moment to gaze deeply into his eyes.

"Yes, I think you're right," she whispered at last. "I think you understand me very well."

Then, sliding her hands around his neck, she lifted her face for another kiss.

"And *I* think it's time you two went home."

Chapter Six

Martha Lawrence stood a few feet away. She'd put her apron back on and carried a plastic trash sack in one hand and what remained of a slice of wedding cake in the other. Having said her piece, she popped it into her mouth and licked white and pink icing from her fingers.

"That's not a bad idea," Michael said, approving of her candor as much as her logic. He gently grasped Blair by her shoulders. "It is a long drive."

"Not that long," Blair tossed back before narrowing her eyes at her mother. "Stop meddling, Mother, and what are you doing? The band is about ready to play again and you still have guests who want to party. You can't start cleaning up. Besides, when you do, I intend to help."

"Am I chasing anyone away?"

"What was that suggestion just now?" Blair asked her dryly.

"Well, shoot. What was I supposed to say when you're under here scorching my prize Don Juans?"

"Mother!"

"Anyway, I don't need any more help," the older woman continued, ignoring Blair's indignation. "Violet's staying over. You know I don't like too many females in my kitchen at any one time. Mike, honey, it was a real pleasure. Don't be a stranger."

As she walked away Michael chuckled softly. "I could become a big fan of hers."

"She's incorrigible," muttered Blair, still feeling the heat of embarrassment in her cheeks.

"Just because she voiced what we were thinking?" He gently turned Blair to face him and framed her face with his hands. "So she doesn't sugarcoat her words. What she said was the truth. We want to be alone, don't we?"

How could she think straight when he was seducing her with his eyes, reminding her of how good it felt to be touched by caressing her cheeks with his thumbs? She sighed wistfully. "I'd like that, Michael, but I don't want to give you the wrong idea. I mean, I'm not ready for anything more than—"

"Kissing?" he murmured, lowering his head to brush his lips against hers. "Touching?" He slowly drew his fingers down the length of her neck and lightly massaged the stiffness in the taut muscles at her nape.

"Yes," she whispered, letting her eyelids drift shut as her body defied her mind and tempted her to enjoy everything she could experience with this man.

Michael could feel her vulnerability, and it filled him with a sense of elation and joy. "That's all I want, too. How else are we going to get to know one another and build a basis of trust?"

He was right. Taking a deep breath, Blair opened her eyes and, smiling, nodded. "All right. Let's go."

Though the interior of Blair's car was white, they found it was still incredibly hot when they climbed inside. But it worked to their advantage as their preoccupation with starting the engine and turning on the air conditioner took care of the anticipatory silence that had begun to settle between them.

"Now that the wedding's over with, we could use a quick downpour," Michael said, tugging at his tie and unbuttoning his collar.

Blair scooped her hair up off her neck and fanned herself with her other hand. "I wouldn't even mind a mini-blue norther."

"A blue norther and golf ball-size hail."

"Wait a minute. Let's find an underpass for this thing before you wish us that."

Michael indicated the hazy but cloudless sky through the windshield. "Unless you've offended some deity lately, I think you're safe."

They continued to indulge in that aimless chatter until they were back on the highway where they happened upon another car bearing the white lettering Just Married and an assortment of other less tame remarks. Streamers of white crepe paper were tied to the radio antenna, door handles and bumper, while the couple inside sat so close they could easily have been sharing the same seat belt.

"In comparison, your brother and Alicia got off easy." Michael said, as they passed the car.

"It helped to inform everyone that they were flying to their honeymoon destination and that a friend was using his own car to drive them to the airport," Blair said. "But his best man told me that they're going to get them when they leave for California."

Michael glanced over to see her amused, contented smile. "Did you have a good time?"

"Dare I say it? I did. Did you?"

Wanting to touch her he reached over to take her hand as he had before and was pleased to note that this time she curled her fingers around his. "Couldn't you tell?"

"You might just be a terrific actor," she teased. When he shot her a strange look, she felt compelled to apologize. "I didn't mean to suggest you were, I only meant that considering how unpredictable these family gatherings can be, it would be understandable if you'd ended up less than thrilled with the experience."

"I'm thrilled with *you*." He lifted her hand to his lips for a fleeting kiss.

Blair knew she came close to jabbering the rest of the way home. She was almost grateful when, upon pulling up into her driveway an hour later, Michael shut off the engine, reached over to unlock both their seat belts, then unerringly locked his mouth to hers.

"Nerves are lousy things," he murmured against her lips long moments later.

He *did* understand. "Why is it that I can walk into a meeting with a client and have all the confidence in the world, challenge my bosses, but with you I regress back to being as awkward as an eighteen-year-old on a blind date?"

"Because you've never felt like this with anyone before," he replied, drawing her closer and brushing her hair back from her face. "Neither have I. It's understandable that it should be a bit frightening."

"I stop being frightened when you kiss me," she heard herself whisper.

With a smile in his eyes, Michael lowered his head once again. Blair stretched to meet him halfway. It felt wonderful. Her lips touched his the same instant her breasts met his hard chest. Both meetings were tenuous yet provocative. Both made her want so much more.

Michael provided that by splaying his hands across her back and drawing her more firmly against him while simultaneously parting her lips for a deeper, more tantalizing kiss. This time he held nothing of his feelings and needs back. The moment was right, she was willing and, dear heavens, he *needed* to hold her like this.

He wanted to absorb her. She was supple and smooth, making him think of days as a boy when his family had taken a rare trip to the Gulf and he'd spent hours on a raft floating above the soothing ocean waves. He'd felt invincible then, yet serene. She brought him those same feelings; yet like that ocean she wasn't quite tame. The nip of her teeth on his jaw and the bite of her short nails into his nape made his heart thrum with excitement at that discovery.

His body heated as rapidly as the air in their close confine. Still he leaned back against the driver's door and drew her with him. He wanted more, to feel all of her, to feel her heart beating wildly against his. He wanted to know—

A beeping jerked him back to reality with an unpleasant swiftness.

"What's that?" Blair asked, straightening her clothes even as he eased her to her side of the car.

There was no way he could avoid telling her. "My beeper."

She began to question whether she'd heard him correctly when he reached inside his coat and drew out the small receiver that had been attached to his belt. Was that why he hadn't removed his jacket all day? Surely not. What difference did it make if anyone knew he carried one?

Looking from it back to him she didn't know what to say. She didn't want to insult him, but it didn't make sense. It never occurred to her that his was the type of work that required him to be on call.

"I suppose we'd better go inside so you can call," she said, already glancing around to see where her purse had landed.

"No. I'd better report in."

"*Report in?*"

"They wouldn't have paged me if it wasn't important."

"Right," she said slowly, "Umm . . . what do you suppose is wrong?"

"The sprinkler system at the greenhouse," he said, grabbing at the first thing that came to mind. "Ah— we've been having problems with it in the past few days. It runs on timers. Very sensitive stuff. They told me they'd have to call me in if it broke down again." He couldn't decide what bothered him more, lying to her or having to leave her. "I'd better get going."

"Of course." A little bewildered, she brushed a hand over her hair, dislodging the rose he'd placed there earlier. Seeing it reminded her of something else. "Oh, wait."

He turned back from the door in time to see her sliding her skirt up a few inches and removing the garter. "Thanks," he murmured gruffly, accepting it from her. It carried her body's warmth and he gripped it even tighter. "For everything."

"You're welcome."

"I really did have a good time."

"I'm glad. So did I."

"Good enough to try it again?"

"One small problem . . . I only have one brother."

Relaxing, Michael smiled and slipped his hand behind her head to draw her close. "I mean a date. A real one. You, me and intimate but unthreatening intentions."

"I think I'd like that," she whispered, caught up in the secret messages she read in his eyes.

"Then I'll be in touch."

Because he knew if he kissed her again he wouldn't be able to leave her, Michael forced himself out of her car and went to see why he had been summoned to headquarters.

"And then what happened?"

"I imagine that Eloise beat everyone who challenged her, though we didn't hang around to watch," Blair told Tess. "Arm wrestling has never been one of my favorite spectator sports."

"But it went well with Michael?" her secretary asked, eager to hear everything. "You're not sorry you asked him to go?"

No, she wasn't sorry, but neither was she ready to divulge her complex inner feelings. "He's a nice man."

"Nice enough to go out with again?"

With a brief laugh Blair pointed toward the door of her office. "Go! I need that memo we discussed before lunch."

As Tess wrinkled her nose and left, Blair sat back in her chair and shook her head. Poor Michael. He was undoubtedly going to be grilled, too, unless she could think of a reason to send Tess on an errand when he came in later.

At the thought of Michael she began to check her watch, only to realize she wasn't wearing it. She'd been late leaving the house that morning and had carried it with her to put on in the car. Instead she'd laid it on the dashboard, forgetting all about it.

"Mondays." She sighed, getting her keys out of her purse and pushing herself to her feet. Things could only get better. Knowing she dare not leave the expensive piece of jewelry where it was, she hurried out of her office.

"Tess, I'm going down to my car for a minute. I forgot my watch and I don't want to tempt anyone to break in and help themselves to it."

"If Michael comes while you're gone, do you want me to tell him to have a seat and wait for you?" she asked with a grin.

"Not funny, Tess. Not funny at all."

But Blair was smiling when she stepped from the elevator into the lobby. She *was* looking forward to seeing him again. Truth be known, she'd expected him to call as early as yesterday. She wasn't quite ready to admit that that was why she'd turned Seth down on his invitation to attend a poetry reading and stayed home to dust and repaper her kitchen drawers; but she would allow that she'd been slightly disappointed when she'd crawled into bed Sunday night without having heard from Michael. Well, at least the drawers got done, she reminded herself as she hurried across the street and into the parking garage.

It felt good to get out of the sun even though she was wearing white and the silk shift was cool. A car passed her and started up the ramp to the next level. Its squealing tires made her wince and glance over in its direction. Seeing Michael in the Lone Star Plantscaping station wagon made her do a double take.

As she approached him, she saw that he was wearing earphones and alternately fiddling with them and then with something in the car. A radio? Since when did he play a radio on the job?

"Michael?" Knowing he couldn't hear her, she touched his shoulder.

He spun around. His quick reflexes once again reminded her of the night he'd defended them against the would-be mugger in the restaurant alley.

"Blair." He ripped off the earphones and tossed them behind him. Then he got out of the car and quickly shut the door. "What are you doing here?"

"I didn't mean to startle you, but I was about to ask you the same thing. Moonlighting as a detective or something?"

He stared at her without blinking. "Why do you say that?"

"You know—earphones, surveillance," she said, embarrassed that her joke fell flat. "Is your radio giving you problems?"

"My radio... yes. But I think it's only weak batteries."

"Oh, well, what kind do you use?" She shifted around him to get a better look into the car. "I usually keep some extras in my desk. Maybe they'll fit."

Instead of replying, Michael slipped his arms around her waist and spun her around so that she had her back to the car. "Forget the batteries," he said, pressing his mouth to hers.

Within seconds Blair was feeling feverish and lightheaded. Each time they kissed her reaction was growing more intense. But why shouldn't she enjoy a man kissing her? she thought with an inner sigh of contentment.

Because Michael isn't any man.

He wouldn't rush her into anything she didn't want. He understood she needed time and lots of space.

You're already rubber legged and his hands are still in a safe zone.

But even as she thought that, they began to move. He began to caress her back, slowly inching them downward...

Blair broke the kiss, gently pushing against his chest. "Michael—we're in a public place."

The crooked smile that came to his lips as he glanced around and realized she was right made her instantly forgive him, even wish they could go somewhere more private. The thought sent little alarm bells ringing down the vacated corridors that once housed her common sense.

"Sorry." He sighed, reluctantly allowing her to ease herself out of his arms. "What brought you out here? Are you going to a meeting or something?"

"No. I came down to get my watch. I forgot it in the car. Then I saw you and thought I'd come over and say hello. Michael, it's none of my business, but you're not going to get into trouble for playing that radio while on the job, are you?"

He gave her an indifferent shrug. "I don't turn it on unless I'm sure no one is around who'll report me."

Blair wasn't sure she approved of that attitude and decided to change the subject. "How did the rest of the weekend go?" she asked, though seconds before she told herself not to bring it up. "The sprinklers, I mean. Did you get the problem fixed?"

"Eventually," he murmured, admiring the way her dress flattered her figure and her complexion. "Temporarily. I missed you," he added, reaching out to touch her hair.

So much that you couldn't resist calling?

A car passed them. It was someone Blair recognized who had an office on McGowan and Birch's floor. It reminded her that someone from her own office could come by at any moment.

"I'd better get back upstairs before Tess sends out a search party." She took a step backward, waiting for him to say something. Anything. "See you later."

He smiled, but stopped short of verbally committing himself. He couldn't make any promises. Something had come up and there was work to do.

Though the smile was nice, she expected more. But the invitation didn't happen and, feeling confused and more than a little disappointed she turned and hurried to her car.

The next time she saw him was Wednesday in the lobby. It wasn't his normal day for rounds, but as she soon discerned, he was waiting for the service elevator so he could deliver a new plant to one of his clients.

Blair took it as kismet. They'd never had a chance to talk again Monday because she'd been called into a meeting and by the time she got back to her office, Tess told her Michael had already come and gone. At the time she told herself it was for the best, that she needed to keep her thoughts focused on business and that this made it easier for her.

But on Wednesday morning Roger McGowan stopped her on his way out of town and gave her his two tickets to the opening of one of the season's summer musicals at Fair Park. The moment she saw Michael she knew she didn't want to ask anyone but him to go with her.

"Maybe I should have ordered one of those instead of a tray of cactus," she said, pausing before him.

He slowly straightened from setting the huge cane plant onto its wooden dolly, in the process viewing strappy high-heeled shoes, shapely legs in sheer black hose, a black linen shift and emerald green blazer. "I don't know...it's a bit much for a coffee table. Are you coming or going?"

"Going," she replied, gesturing with her portfolio. "Client meeting. How've you been?"

"Okay. Busy." At least that wasn't a lie. "You?"

"The same." It was true enough, but she knew she would have said it even if wasn't. There was something wrong. His obvious lack of enthusiasm was leaving her with a feeling that he was having second thoughts about things.

"The newlyweds get back from their honeymoon all right?"

"Yes. They leave for California in a few days."

"That's nice." The service elevator arrived and Michael shot her a rueful look. "I'd better get this monster upstairs."

"I need to be going myself." She took a step backward, then retraced the step. "Michael...my boss gave me two tickets to the Fair Park musical tonight. Would you like to go?"

Would the Cowboys like to get out of their slump? Would anyone who travels on Central Expressway like city officials to get off their backsides and *do* something progressive about the transit system? Would both their mothers like to add their ten cents into this conversation? Michael swore silently at the work that forced him to do what he was about to do.

"I can't, Blair," he muttered, looking away. "I have to work tonight."

Was it her imagination or did he sound guilty?

Well, he wouldn't be the first person ever to have experienced a change of heart. And you could have saved yourself a ton of embarrassment if you hadn't been so slow in picking up on it.

But what about that kiss in the garage on Monday? He'd said he'd missed her. Or could it be that he'd just been trying to be a gentleman and let her down gently? Maybe she'd been fooling herself; maybe a quick fling is what he'd had in mind all along, and if she wasn't going to deliver...

Drawing herself erect she gave him a bright smile. "No problem. It was only a passing thought. Listen, I'd better dash or I'm going to be late."

"Blair."

She pretended she didn't hear him. Her heels clicking cheerfully on the marble floor, she hurried across the lobby and out the revolving doors.

By Friday she was telling herself she'd done the right thing and that her life was back into its normal grove. Yesterday she'd accompanied John to a Republican fund-raiser at the Anatole and next week she would attend an anniversary party for Walt's district manager and the manager's wife. She won a new account and lost three pounds without even trying. She should have been on top of the world. But when Tess came into her office to discuss her own plans for the weekend, Blair was confronted with the realization that at best, her spirits could only be described as mediocre.

"Do you think I should be daring and go with the shirred black or stick with demure and wear the cream lace?" Tess asked, ticking off her narrowed down dress choices for what she'd already explained was a major event in her life. "I know she's Kent's sister and it's not the same as meeting his parents, but you *know* she'll phone home and report everything. I have to make a good impression."

Blair frowned down at the photographs of six models on her desk. One was supposed to represent a new client's skin care line, but try as she might, she couldn't get excited over any of them. "Wear what you look best in," she replied absently.

"That's the cream, but it also makes me look five years younger."

"We should all have such problems."

"I want to look my age and like—you know—good wife material."

"What's wrong with just being yourself?"

With a frustrated sigh Tess sat down on the corner of Blair's desk. "You *know* what I mean." She glanced down at the spread of photos and pointed to her favorite. "I love her eyes."

"Mmm . . . nice, but in this case too exotic."

"How about her?" She indicated the brunette on the bottom row.

"Too thin."

"How about me?"

"It's a possibility."

"Here we go again." Tess went over to close Blair's door and, leaning back against it, crossed her arms over her chest. "Okay. What's wrong this time?"

"What are you talking about?"

"You just put me in the running to be the new *Silken Luster* girl. Call me crazy for not grabbing the contract and signing my name on the dotted line, but somehow I don't think you meant what you said."

Blair raked her hands through her already mussed hair and, wanting to avoid her friend's probing look, swiveled her chair toward the window. "Sorry. I guess my mind's not on my work today."

"Lately," Tess corrected. "And since we're making a list, neither is your heart."

"Maybe I'm coming down with a flu or something." She stood and looked down at Thanksgiving Square. The sprinklers were running, sprouting geometric patterns of water over emerald green patches of grass. A faint rainbow hovered above the mist. It was a photogenic image but one that did nothing for her disposition. "Maybe I need a break. Can you remember when I'm scheduled for my vacation?"

"August...and now I *am* worried. Usually you care so much you tell them to write you in somewhere and then you have to be reminded the Friday before not to show up for the next two weeks. What's happened? No, don't tell me. It's Michael, isn't it? You had a fight. Oh, Blair! Not already?"

"No, we haven't fought."

"Then everything's all right between the two of you?"

"I didn't say that, either. In fact I wish I'd never let you talk me into asking him to the wedding. I *thought* it had turned out well. I *thought* we'd had a good time."

Entirely confused, Tess shook her head. "I don't get it."

Blair spun around, her hands on her hips, her eyes flashing with hurt and temper. "Damn it all, he got me interested in him, and now he's dumped me."

"You're kidding. Are you sure?"

"If I can interpret body language in a business meeting and Marvin Birch's 'Hmm's and 'Aha's' in our staff meetings, I think I can tell when a man is trying to avoid me."

"But it doesn't make sense," Tess insisted. "I've told you before, I've seen the way Michael looks at you. The man's got it bad."

"Here's a news bulletin—someone's slipped him an antidote."

"You had to have misinterpreted something."

"You think so? Before I gave you and Kent those tickets the other night, I invited Michael to go with me. He turned me down."

"Did he have an excuse?"

"He *said* he had to work."

"The rat. And you let him get away with that? Oops," she said a second later as Blair glared at her.

"The point is he had the whole week to call me and he hasn't. Fine." She returned to her desk. "I didn't need this kind of hassle in my life anyway." She re-aligned the photos on her desk. "What's more, I don't *want* it, and I'd appreciate you remembering that next time you're tempted to play matchmaker.''

A knock at the door kept Tess from responding. She went to answer it and found Michael standing there. "If it isn't poetic justice," she murmured, moving aside to let him enter. "Come on in, but may I suggest you tread carefully. The natives are carrying big sticks today."

Michael glanced over at Blair. "Was that a round-about way of saying I should come back later?"

"Not at all," Blair replied formally, determined to ignore how good he looked in his navy polo shirt and jeans.

Michael set his tray on the coffee table and began unscrewing a water jug. He, too, was acutely aware. But more than noting the snappy navy-and-white suit she was wearing, he tuned in on the prim set to her ordinarily seductive lips. He also had the uncomfortable feeling that a good portion of the arctic undercurrents in the room were directed at him.

"How was the musical the other night?" he asked, pouring a portion of the jug's contents into the weeping fig's pot.

"I wouldn't know. Something came up so I gave the tickets to Tess."

Not icy currents, Michael amended; frigid. "I thought maybe you might have asked someone else to go."

Blair held up the brunette's photo and glared holes into it. "I would have, but as I said, I was busy."

Michael took his time checking the other plants, ending by the cactus arrangement. Deciding it should skip a watering, he replaced the cap on his jug and set it back in his tray. "Do you want me to go or are you ready to talk?" he finally asked, wiping his hands on a rag.

"Is there a problem with one of the plants?" she replied, purposely misunderstanding him.

Like Tess before him, Michael walked over to the door and shut it. But unlike her, he returned to Blair's desk where, placing his palms flat on the blotter, he leaned over so that they were nearly nose to nose.

"Fact number one—I really did have to work the other night. Fact two—I *have* been busy all this week, it's not some game I'm playing to stir your juices. And fact three—I want to kiss you so badly right now my stomach's in knots."

Blair had to swallow to find her voice. "Michael, maybe this isn't a good idea after all. I've had time to think about it and—"

"You think entirely too much."

"Nevertheless, I believe that it would be best if we stopped things here, before we get involved."

He angled his head and lowered his eyes to her mouth. "I disagree. In fact, I think we're already involved."

"One date—outing does not constitute a relationship," she mumbled, glancing away.

"Do you kiss everyone on your 'outings' the way you kissed me? Make that soft yearning sound? Press your body against them?"

Blair felt as if the air was being sucked from her lungs. "Of course not! It just—" She was going to say *happened* but that would have been a lie. "It was a mistake."

"I'm going out to my place tomorrow to check on things," he continued as if she hadn't spoken. "I thought I'd take a picnic lunch." He leaned forward a little more and lightly touched his lips to her ear. "Want to come along?"

"No."

This time he touched his tongue to the spot. "Sure?"

"Michael!"

"I know. This is your office and you have an image to uphold. But desperate men sometimes have to resort to desperate measures to get their point across. Mine is that I *do* want to be with you. So I'm asking you again, will you come tomorrow?"

She could feel her determination slipping and uttered a sound of frustration. "I wish you'd try to understand."

"I do, believe me. All you have to do is think of one thing," he whispered, capturing her chin and forcing her to face him. He kissed her gently. "Think of the good time we had last Saturday. Now look at me . . . and tell me you don't want to see me again."

How could she do that when his slightest touch sent her heart skittering. Then he kissed her and she knew she was lost. She closed her eyes accepting her weakness.

"All right," she whispered.

She could feel his smile against her lips as he brushed his lips against hers a final time.

"I'll pick you up at eight. Dress in grubbies so I can give you a tour of the place."

The moment he was gone Tess stuck her head into her office. "Mmmhmm. I see you told him a thing or two."

Blair ripped a page off her desk calendar, crumpled it into a ball and threw it at her.

Chapter Seven

Y ou call that grubby?'' Michael asked as Blair opened her door to him the following morning.

She glanced down at her sleeveless, camel-colored jumpsuit and matching moccasins before considering his stone-washed jeans, University of Oklahoma T-shirt and boots. "I call it comfortable. Anyway, to each his own. Do I need to bring anything? Mosquito repellent? Fly swatter? My hospitalization card?''

Michael shifted his hands to his hips. "Are you sure you grew up on a farm?''

"You think a neophyte would ask these questions? Imagine it—at this very moment every species of insect and reptile out there is headed for the nearest watering hole to wash their four, six, eight or one hundred little paws in preparation of the feast— namely us—about to be delivered to them.''

"Nothing like approaching this with an open mind. You aren't by any chance a fan of science fiction novels?"

"Not exactly, but last Mother's Day when Tim and I asked my mother what she wanted, she said a VCR and tapes of both *Alien* movies. She insisted we stay to watch them with her, and I have to admit I found the parallels between my years on the farm and Ripley's in her spaceship eerie."

Michael nodded as if he understood, then tugged her door shut behind her and, slipping his arm around her shoulders, led her to his truck. "There's nothing sorrier than a bad loser."

"Who's a loser, bad or otherwise?"

"You think you were, when you gave in and agreed to come with me today. You've decided to punish us both for your impulsiveness by not having a good time."

Blair was slightly peeved at his insight and noticing she also stood a good five inches shorter than him thanks to her moccasins, stubbornly lifted her chin. "I have not. I'll have you know I can be a very open-minded person."

"Good, because I forgot to mention that you're going to be sharing the front seat with Rocket and he has to sit by the window or he gets car sick."

Before Blair could voice her question regarding who or what a *Rocket* was, she looked into the truck's half-opened passenger window and met the equally pensive eyes of a basset hound. She recognized the look immediately; it was the same one Walt's children wore before they believed she was telling the truth that she and their father were and would remain *only friends*. How did one convince a possessive dog that you weren't a threat to its happy home?

"The question is, is it going to let me in at all?" she asked dryly.

"I'd rather not take the chance of *his* jumping out. Would you mind getting in on my side and sliding over?"

Blair did that, but upon her first full view of Michael's dog, she wondered at his concern. "I don't think you need be overly worried about old Rocket here getting far. In fact I'd wager his sprinting days are far behind him."

Giving her an offended look Rocket eased himself down to the floorboard, squeezed himself between her legs and the seat and wrestled his way onto Michael's lap. With a take-that look for Blair, he rested his head on the frame of the driver's opened window and expelled a belly-deep sigh.

"Sensitive, isn't he?" she murmured. She liked animals well enough; however, Tim had been the one in the family who possessed the great rapport with all creatures great and small.

Michael wryly admitted his pet was slightly possessive. "But it's not really his fault that he's a b-l-i-m-p. He just has a hard time avoiding Harry and her cookies. Harriet Hooper," he explained upon noticing Blair's sidelong look, "My neighbor, the local clearinghouse for all gossip and the major source for tooth decay in the greater Dallas area."

"I wasn't doubting you. I was wondering at the necessity of s-p-e-l-l-i-n-g."

"He's very sensitive about his you-know-what."

As he started the truck Blair looked for a twinkle in his eye, a twitch to his lips. Spotting neither, she decided she'd done the right thing in not getting a pet for herself. Apparently they had a strange effect on otherwise completely sane people.

While buckling her seatbelt she noticed his glasses case on the seat between them. Not again, she thought; but this time, rather than scold him, she simply took them out of their case and slipped them on her own nose.

"Good grief," she muttered a moment later. She glanced over the rims and then through the lenses again. "You weren't joking about these being a weak prescription. They're like clear glass. Why did you let the doctor stick you with them?"

"I'm a sucker for people just starting out in business, and he looked like he needed the money."

He was joking—wasn't he? Not sure what to make of it, she put the glasses back in their case. "Well, I'm sorry I gave you such a hard time last week."

"If you really want to apologize, you'd slide over and use the middle safety belt."

Blair eyed Rocket sitting contentedly in his lap. "I think you have your hands full as it is," she drawled and settled back in her seat.

Saturday traffic was light and Michael made good time driving through town and around LBJ Freeway. When he turned off on Highway 175, both he and Blair had to adjust their sun visors against the glare of the sun.

"Want to hear something strange?" she asked, peering at the receding skyline of Dallas in the truck's sideview mirror. "In about five seconds I'm going to be lost. I've never driven farther east than Mesquite before."

"Disgraceful—and you call yourself a native? You mean you've never gone to First Monday in Canton and haggled over the price of something you couldn't live without with an antiques or collectibles vendor? Or visited Tyler during their Azalea Trails or Rose Festival? Or driven the old time railroad down in Rusk? Or cut your own Christmas tree at one of the countless tree farms?"

Brushing her windswept hair from her face, Blair laughed at the way he was making her sound. "Do I get any brownie points for faithfully fulfilling my voting responsibilities?"

It pleased him greatly to hear her laugh again, but Michael worked hard on keeping a straight face. "No doubt about it, Miss Lawrence. I came into your life just in time."

Torn between agreeing with him and worrying *how* important he could become to her, Blair turned back to watch the passing scenery.

Somewhere north of Cedar Creek Lake Michael turned onto a two lane farm-to-market road and traffic became all but nonexistent. The scenery changed, too, and Blair found herself quickly warming to the rolling terrain—so different from where she'd grown up—and the lushness and diversity of the vegetation. Maybe if her mother had decided to establish a farm someplace like this, perhaps she wouldn't have been so eager to leave the life.

The thought startled her and she glanced at Michael, hoping he hadn't noticed anything amiss. "What made you choose to buy land out here?" she asked him.

"Lots of things—the beauty of it, the plentiful rainfall and mild winters..." But those were the sensible answers, he mused and he searched deeper in his heart to give her as much honesty as he could.

"It's a place of peace and privacy. You can work a piece of land and not see another soul for days. If you're hankering for news, you need only drive over to the nearest country store and catch up on all the local gossip. Everybody knows everybody out here, but no one bothers you unless you invite it. The Caddo Indians knew that, and a fair amount of renegades found it a fair hiding place as well. A lot of people came out here to make a new life for themselves. I like the history in that, to sit under a old oak and wonder what it's seen in its time."

"That's a very romantic answer."

"I'm a very romantic guy."

The words were teasing, but there was no missing the caress in his soft-as-suede voice. Blair felt as if he'd reached over and brushed his lips across her cheek. "So," she said, her voice slightly breathless, "when do we get to this oasis of serenity?"

"In about—hold on!"

They'd just come around a sharp bend when a doe leaped out from the woods and raced across the road. Michael hit his brakes, simultaneously clutching

Rocket to his chest. Blair grabbed the dashboard but even so, and despite her seat belt, she lurched forward. Her knees hit the glove compartment and it bounced open.

As the deer disappeared into the woods on the opposite side of the road, Michael soothed his dog and shot a quick glance at Blair. "Are you okay?"

She'd been more interested in the doe's safety, but rubbing her knee she nodded. "More startled than anything else. I think I might have dented your—" Looking down for the first time, she saw the gun in the glove compartment. "Michael . . . why?"

Though he'd known the question was going to come up the instant he saw the glove compartment door open, and silently chastised himself for not locking it, he took a moment or two to pretend a preoccupation with adjusting Rocket in his lap and concentrating on the road. "Snakes," he said at last, using the most plausible explanation he could think of. "I ran across a timber rattler out there not long ago—big sucker, almost five feet long and as big around as my arm— and there's always an occasional copperhead or water moccasin. Never hurts to be prepared."

Having no great affection for snakes, Blair nodded again and shut the door. Even her mother had a shotgun around for such situations. Only she hoped Michael was an exemplary shot; if she had to face a snake the size he'd described, she would want something guaranteed not to miss—like a bazooka.

Michael soon turned onto another narrow road and minutes later pointed to a new barbed wire fence up ahead. "That's the beginning of my place," he told her.

He'd been right about it being primarily wooded land, Blair thought, eyeing the solid mass of pine and hardwood trees just inside the fire line he'd cut. But what impressed her more was the distance it was to his front gate. "How 'small' did you say this was?" she asked suspiciously.

As he shifted into park to go unlock the gate, he shrugged. "About two hundred forty some odd acres."

Blair watched him walk to the galvanized steel gate and shook her head. Her mother's place was barely sixty and she'd thought it was too big for the three of them to handle. When Michael returned a moment later, she told him that. "And you said you were going to give me a tour of this place? You did mean drive, didn't you?"

"Not exactly."

"I don't care if a bear walks out of these woods," Blair moaned hours later, as she sprawled back on the blanket Michael had just spread out for them. "I'm not taking another step unless it's to the truck."

Michael lifted the ice chest out of the back of the truck and set it on one corner of the blanket before dropping down beside her. "There hasn't been any bear in these parts for years." Lifting the lid he drew out two beers and offered her one. "Try this. It might revive you."

"Bless you." Raising herself on her elbow, Blair first rolled the can across her forehead. She closed her eyes, enjoying the coolness against her feverish skin, but she was parched, as well. Popping the tab, she concentrated on quenching her thirst.

Michael took a few gulps of his own beer, then leaned back. Their shoulders were almost touching and he reached out to brush her hair behind her ear. He liked her this way, with her cheeks flushed and her eyes sparkling from the lively banter they'd shared during their walk. She always looked beautiful to him, but now there was an almost serene expression in her eyes and that induced a beauty all its own.

"So, what do you think of the place?"

"It's big."

"You've already said that."

"I wanted to make sure you heard me."

"I did back when we first crossed the creek at the northeast boundary, then again when we trekked up that hill that overlooked that small back meadow, and again when I showed you the beaver dam in the south section." He watched her take another drink, admiring the starkness of her lashes against her skin and the smooth column of her throat. "I think you liked the beaver dam best, but it's a flood zone in the spring and fall—too risky to build a house."

Blair almost choked and shot him a wary look. "No, umm, I wouldn't want to hear your house got flooded."

"I was leaning toward this meadow myself. In the spring there's an abundant variety of wildflowers and it seems most of the dogwood are in this area."

"Well, it's your land, Michael," Blair said, giving serious concentration to the task of wiping moisture from the can. "You should build wherever you want."

"But I'd want you to like it, too. After all, how am I going to get you to come out here with me, if you're not happy here?"

He was so charming about it, his expression so boyishly innocent, that her wariness turned to amusement. "Don't you ever give up?"

"What, now when I'm on a roll? Two weeks ago you barely knew I existed. You paid as much attention to me as you do those plants in your office."

"You make me sound delightful."

"You are, but it's a side of you people have to work at uncovering. Fortunately for you, I like peeling away the layers." He dropped his gaze and slowly drew his finger down the length of her arm, as if he were removing that first, fragile layer.

Feeling that familiar tingling sensation, Blair began to sit up, but Michael held her back. In the next instant he set aside his beer and then placed hers beside it.

"You can't keep running, Blair," he murmured, releasing her arm to tuck her hair behind her ear. "And there's no need. I only want to hold you. Kiss you. I know you're not ready for anything more. Besides, the first time we make love, I want it to be on a big comfortable bed with cool crisp sheets and lots of time."

As he leaned forward and ran a series of fleeting kisses across her cheek, Blair felt as if a blossom was unfolding within her chest, but the warmth it spread hadn't yet sedated her mind. "Michael, you make it so difficult for me to stay sensible about this."

"What have I told you about thinking too much?" He cupped his hand around the back of her head and closed his mouth over hers, intent on remedying the problem himself.

She stiffened, and accepted the inevitability of that, Michael drew on his long experience with patience to wait for her to relax. She'd worked on her defenses since the first time he kissed her, but rather than it disturbing him, he found it reassuring. If she didn't care, she wouldn't resist him. If he didn't touch her on some deep level, she wouldn't feel vulnerable. Someday, somehow he would learn more about why she kept a padlock on her heart, but first she had to accept that he wasn't going to go away. Ever.

The melting came slowly, like dawn on a frost-bitten meadow. He savoured it as if he were a man long lost in the dark. The analogy didn't slip by him and he found it fitting. The days when he could work in the darkness—enjoy the solitude, accept the restrictions his job inflicted on his life—were over. Finding the dawn, finding Blair, was a gift he hadn't expected and one he intended to cherish.

It hurt, she thought, feeling a burning behind her closed lids. The care and patience with which he kissed her had a sweetness to it and made her ache inside, crumbling her defenses with an ease that was stunning. How wonderous to feel like this, if only for a few moments.

With a soft sigh she parted her lips, beckoning him to share more of his warmth with the touch of her fingers against his smooth-shaven cheek. She could feel his reaction, the slight shudder that shook the hands holding her so carefully; then the mounting desire as he made a deeper exploration, his tongue moving over hers, sharing, asking.

He needed more. He eased her back against the sun-warmed blanket without breaking the kiss, and slowly stretched out beside her. But even he couldn't anticipate how good it would feel to be touching her from head to toe, to realize that she wanted this just as much as he did. It ignited a fire within him like a match to a parched field and, uttering something unintelligible, he buried his face in her hair and crushed her to him.

"Michael . . ."

"Shh . . . I know."

She could feel his heart pounding like hers, feel the growing need in him that only intensified her own fever, short-circuiting every thought but those of him. She wanted him. She told him with her hands as she massaged his taut neck muscles and restlessly slid them down his hot, damp back; she told him with the fleeting kisses she awarded his hair, his neck, his shoulder.

Michael arched against her gifted touch and began an exploration of his own. She was sleek and smooth beneath his hands, her curves making him wish he were a sculptor so he could capture her forever in marble. But he didn't really need a statue to remind himself of her perfection, because she belonged to him and he never intended to let her go.

"Kiss me," he whispered against her lips. "Hard."

She did, wrapping her arms around his neck and pressing herself against him. Nothing, she thought, had ever felt this good. But when he slid his hand up her side and he covered her breast, she realized that he was only beginning to show her how good it could be between them.

"I want to see you," he said, his voice low and gruff with desire. Slowly he eased her onto her back and reached between them for the zipper on her jumpsuit.

Mesmerized, Blair didn't consider stopping him, even though she'd always been self-conscious about the way men had a tendency to stare at her chest. She was caught in his magic and she wanted to know how much more pleasure was possible.

As he drew the zipper down to her waist, the sun heated her skin even more, but no more than the silver flames in his eyes as he peeled back the bodice and looked at her. Her bra was sheer and she knew, as she felt her nipples tighten, that it hid little from his intense scrutiny. But even she wasn't prepared for the scorching heat that inflamed her when he flicked open the front catch and lowered his mouth to her.

She closed her eyes, felt her breath lock in her throat. Pleasure and pain mingled, becoming one. Feeling something wild, primitive take hold of her she arched her back off the blanket and asked for more.

He'd dreamed of them like this, only reality was better—and sheer hell on his good intentions. Yet he needed a moment of indulgence because he'd been hungry for so long. But finally, he knew he'd pushed himself as far as he dare go. Shifting to once again bury his face in her hair, he crushed her against him.

"No more," he rasped.

She couldn't have replied if she'd wanted to. Her mind was too dazed to think, her body buzzing from the barrage of sensations. Blair stroked her hand down his back, acutely aware of his unsatisfied need.

"Michael, this is so much more difficult for you."

"I'll be all right in a minute."

"You make me feel things I've never felt before."

He closed his eyes in sweet agony. "Maybe you'd better not say anything else for a few minutes."

Aware he was trying to lighten the mood between them, she summoned a soft laugh. "You know you would recover more easily if you'd let go."

He did, reluctantly, and watched with possessive eyes as she demurely turned away and adjusted her clothes. Knowing he needed to hear her admit that they had achieved a new point in their relationship, he sat up and, as she began to zipper her jumpsuit, slid his hand inside to cup her breast.

"One of these days you're going to let me watch you do that," he murmured, kissing her as he stroked his thumb over her nipple.

Blair couldn't hide the delicious shiver that rushed through her body and she knew he deserved nothing less than her own honesty, as well. "I believe you—or more accurately, I *want* to believe you. But I don't think I'm a candidate for a long-term relationship, Michael."

"You've said as much before. Can you tell me why?"

"There's not much to tell. It's just that my faith in relationships, in *men* isn't very durable. I know if I try to rationalize it, I can trace it back to my father deserting us."

"And you think anyone else you get close to will eventually desert you, too?"

"It's ridiculous, I know. Just putting the feeling into words makes me feel like a fool, but it doesn't make it go away."

Michael leaned forward to kiss her temple. "You're afraid of being hurt again. That's a very human reaction. I wish I could guarantee that I'm never going to say or do something to hurt you—but, Blair, you have to believe that I'm going to try my damndest to avoid it."

She felt a lump rise in her throat and smiled at him through slightly watery eyes. "I think that's what I find most irresistible about you. Your sincerity. But," she murmured dryly. "I can't believe we're having this conversation while your hand is where it is."

Feeling a twinge of guilt Michael dropped his eyes and, giving her a crooked smile, withdrew his hand. "Why—umm—why don't we open that ice chest and concentrate on a different hunger?"

The moment he popped the catch on the lid, Rocket, who'd passed out the moment they arrived back at their picnic site, raised his head expectantly. Blair laughed and shook her head.

"At least I can appreciate *that* reaction. I'm starved."

"Me, too," Michael replied, gazing intently at her profile. However, he was only beginning to realize there were some hungers that would take a lifetime to satisfy.

Chapter Eight

Michael, you're not listening to a word I say.'' Blair sighed as they walked from the parking garage to her building. Pausing a moment for a taxi to speed by, only to have it stop directly in her path, she repressed the urge to say something explicit to the driver and went around it. Even as she went through the revolving doors into her building, Michael was directly behind her.

"Of course I am," he replied. With his long strides, he easily kept up with her on their route toward the elevators. "You've got a full schedule today ending with a client meeting. It sounds as if you'll be ready for a little time for yourself by the end of the day."

They stepped inside an empty car. Pushing the fifth-floor button, Blair leaned back against the black glass wall, grateful for its support. Ready? It was barely seven-thirty on a Monday morning and she already felt *ready*, but only to crawl back under the covers.

In the month since the wedding, her workload had grown to a proportion where she was beginning to wonder how long she could continue the pace. Not only had she acquired several new clients, her associate, Pete Harkness, had recently suffered a heart attack and she'd inherited a number of his accounts for the duration of his recuperation. This morning she felt like putting dibs on the bed beside his.

It was hardly conducive to an evolving romance. Since their trip to Michael's property a few weeks ago, she'd juggled her schedule so she could go out with him several more times, and she had to admit that what was between them was special.

"The only thing I'm going to feel like doing is finding someplace to curl up and pass out," she told him, adding an apologetic smile. "I'm sorry."

"Tell you what, why don't you come over to my place when you can, and not only will I feed you, I'll throw in the world's best neck massage as a bonus."

It sounded wonderful, but Blair knew it wouldn't be fair. "I'll be terrible company."

"No, you won't."

Their arrival at her floor forced her to make a decision. "All right. But you mustn't expect me before seven, okay?"

It was closer to eight when she pulled into Michael's driveway, having barely remembered the way from last week when they'd stopped there for him to run a quick errand. The freshly painted white and brick house with its immaculate yard and Rocket

waddling out from the beneath the breezeway to in-
vestigate gave her a nostalgic feeling of homecoming.

"Hello, tough guy," she murmured, barely able to
get out of the car because the dog rolled onto his back.
She stopped to give him a quick belly rub. "Have you
decided you like me, or will anyone do?"

"What do you think of my security system?" Michael asked, coming to greet her her.

Blair gave the full-bellied dog a final scratch before
straightening. "Impenetrable. Sorry I'm late."

"No problem...though I was beginning to worry
about you." He slid his arms around her waist and
gave her a quick kiss on her temple before leading her
toward the house. "How'd it go?"

"I never thought I'd hear myself say this, but I'd
give anything to be able to disappear for a few days
and unscramble my brain. My *Silken Luster* model
came down with the chicken pox of all things—Pete
Harkness's biggest client doesn't like the Santa Fe
colors I used in his ad...don't get me started," she
said, waving her hand. "It's enough that *I'm* being
driven crazy."

"You know I like to hear about your work."

He led her around back, and they climbed the stairs
to the deck. Blair took a deep breath of the fragrant air
and exhaled with a murmur of approval.

"I love what you've done with this yard. But all
these flowers...it has to be time-consuming to care for
them."

"It's therapy for me," he replied without thinking.

Blair gave him a perplexed look. "You work with
plants all day."

He mentally kicked himself for the slip and gave her a sheepish smile. "You're right, it sounds redundant. I suppose what I meant is that sometimes I get impatient to have my own business. It's going to take a lot more money than I've managed to save so far, but I'm still eager to get started."

"I would think that's only natural," she replied, trying to reassure him. As he held the door open for her and she entered the kitchen, Blair was conscious of a sudden urge to offer to loan him the money.

Easy does it, she reminded herself quickly. They were still feeling their way around each other—offering to help him financially would open the door to a set of problems she wasn't ready to face.

"What's that frown for?" Michael asked, coming up to her and casually sliding his hands up her arms and shoulders to her neck to massage the tense muscles he discovered there.

"Just tired I guess. Mmm...that feels good," she murmured, closing her eyes in rapture.

Unable to resist because he'd been thinking of little else all day, Michael lowered his head and touched his lips to hers. "And that?" he whispered huskily.

"Even better." But as she felt him close in for another kiss, she heard the kitchen door opening behind her. She immediately stiffened and turned to see a small, matronly woman enter.

"Sorry for interrupting, dears, but I wanted to bring over this peach cobbler," Harriet said breezily. Shoving the glass casserole dish into Michael's hands and turning, she extended one hand to Blair. "Hello, I'm glad to finally meet you. I'm Harriet Hooper, and whatever he's told you about me, don't believe it. I'm just a sweet old lady who has more time on her hands than things to do."

"Michael only speaks of you with affection, Mrs. Hooper," Blair replied, shaking her hand.

"You're sweet to say so—unfortunately, I know this big lug." She turned to Michael and drew out an envelope from the pocket of her housedress. "Do you have a minute to look at something for me? It's about Jack's pension. I knew if anyone could understand their jargon you could."

Blair saw Michael's quick glance in her direction and thought he was hesitating because of her. "If you'll excuse me for a moment, I'd like to go wash up while you do that. Which way to the bathroom?"

"Make a right and it's down the hall," Michael replied, giving her a grateful smile. But as soon as she was gone the smile vanished, and he gave his neighbor a look of reproach. "Damn, Harry, what were you thinking of just now?"

"What did I do? Oh! You mean you haven't *told* her yet?" she whispered back. "What are you waiting for, your silver wedding anniversary?"

With another glance toward the hallway, he took her arm and led her back outside. "I know it's past time. But whenever I decide to tell her something comes up. You've seen the papers this week—the stories about the trouble in some of the Central American countries? Well, there's a rumor there might be a retaliation by a rebel faction directed against one of the government's bigwigs during his upcoming visit to the States. You know I can't go into it, but you can appreciate that now's not a good time for Blair to be burdened with the knowledge of my real job.''

Inside, Blair had just rinsed her hands in the bathroom sink and turning to the towel rack, realized it was empty. She settled for blotting her hands in a tissue, but afterward she checked all the cabinets to look for a towel to hang on the empty rack. Finding none, she decided to check for a hallway linen closet.

There were three closed doors in the hallway. From the sounds coming from the one on her left, she knew it only held the water heater, so she tried the nearest door on her right. It was locked.

"Well, how strange," she murmured.

"Get lost?" Michael asked, poking his around the corner of the kitchen.

Startled, Blair gasped. "You always do that!" she chuckled, touching her hand to her chest. "No, I was just looking for a towel to put in the bathroom and noticed this. Did you accidentally lock yourself out of this room?"

"Ah, no. That's my junk room and in order to keep Harry from trying to straighten out the mess when she's cleaning for me, I simply lock it. The towels are in the linen closet one door over. Don't be long, I'm putting dinner on the table."

Sympathetic to Blair's dislike for heavy meals, dinner consisted of a lightly breaded catfish fillet, a salad and scallop potatoes. It was delicious and the time passed quickly with easy conversation.

"You were right, I did need this," she said, when they'd finished their coffee and dessert. But knowing she had another hectic day waiting for her, she told

Michael she was going to have to leave. "I hate to eat and run," she told him, seeing his disappointment. "Let me at least help you with the dishes."

"Don't be silly. That's what dishwashers are for." Rising from his chair, he took her hand and drew her from her seat and into his arms. "Anyway, as much as I hate letting you go, I can see you're exhausted. You need to slow down, Blair. You're going to make yourself ill."

"You're right, but with Pete still recuperating, I don't have much choice."

Michael pretended shock, giving her a wide-eyed stare. "Am I hearing correctly? Blair Lawrence might finally be admitting she's a workaholic?" As she laughed, Michael stroked his hands up and down her back. "Maybe since you're in such a amenable mood, I should press for a few other concessions."

"That's all you're getting, buster. Kiss me good night so I can get out of here."

Not needing a second invitation, Michael claimed her mouth with his, putting his heart and soul into the kiss. Within seconds he could feel Blair melt against him and his body heated with long suppressed needs. Cupping her hips with his hands, he pressed her even closer and deepened the kiss until she needed no translation for what he was asking.

"Michael," Blair whispered, gently pushing against his chest. "I really have to go."

"Stay with me."

"I can't."

"But you want to." He could hear the internal conflict she was experiencing in her voice. It was the only thing that allowed him to keep himself in control and lift his head enough to gaze deeply into her eyes. "When people react to each other the way we do, it's the natural progression of things, sweetheart."

"I know." She touched his cheek, her eyes asking for understanding, "I can't hide the way I feel about you. But I need a little more time, Michael. There's so much pressure on me right now."

More than she realized, Michael thought bitterly. "Too much." He touched his lips to her forehead. "Let me ask you something. Have you ever thought of leaving Dallas, settling down to a quieter life, having a baby?"

Blair tried to label the sudden racing of her heart as surprise, but she knew it was excitement, as well. Just the thought of carrying Michael's baby was incredible... and an unrealistic dream. "You know that I have a job that I love," she reminded him quietly.

"All I can see is that you're working yourself into an early grave. There *is* more to life than your myopic vision is allowing you to see. What about love and marriage?"

"The statistics for longevity don't give it good odds."

"We're human beings, not statistics."

The realization that she wanted to believe him, wanted him to kiss her now and make her mind stop putting up all these roadblocks was almost frightening. Shaking her head she tried to put a fraction more distance between them. "We don't have any business talking about such things, Michael. There's so much we still don't know about each other."

He knew that only too well and the knowledge filled him with frustration. "Well, what do you want me to do? Make a list of my good and bad habits? My clothes size? My astrological sign? Hell, *learning* about each other takes years. It's the commitment that matters!"

Blair backed away from his surge of temper as much as the word *commitment*. "Maybe I'm just not ready for that yet," she murmured sadly.

"Or maybe it's enough for you to make the men in your life pay for your father's mistakes!" As soon as he saw the shock in her eyes, Michael swore and turned away.

"I think it's past time I left," she said, going to collect her purse from the coffee table.

"Blair, we need to talk about this if we're going to overcome it."

"Maybe some other time. Right now I'm tired, I have another horrendous day ahead of me and I'm not in the mood to be analyzed."

Michael caught up with her in the kitchen and grasping her shoulders with a light but firm hand, he turned her to face him. "Don't leave angry."

"I'm not angry."

He gently massaged her rigid shoulder muscles. "You're more tense than you were when you arrived. I don't mean to give you a hard time, but do you have any idea what it does to me to be shut out like this?"

"You're a fine one to talk,' she replied wearily. "You're not exactly a fountain of information about yourself, either."

"I was beginning to think you weren't interested," he murmured, trying to tease her into a better mood.

She eased herself out of his embrace. "Please don't play me for a fool. You're a walking contradiction, Michael. Up until now I haven't said anything because I thought, all right, hoped, this attraction between us might be fleeting. But apparently it's not, and I'll admit I'm worried.

"Sometimes I don't know who you are. Sometimes I'm certain you're keeping things from me. Do you have any idea how frightening that is? I know how deep my scars run, and they're too deep to afford making a big mistake about you. You talk of relationships and commitment and building a basis of trust. Well, I don't know if I trust you, Michael. Good night."

He sent her flowers the following day. Though her eyes filled with tears when she accepted the unique bouquet of bleeding hearts and baby's breath from the messenger, she told Tess to tell him she wasn't in when he phoned later in the afternoon. She knew he would only ask to see her and the cycle would start all over again. She needed time to think. It was becoming more difficult to resist giving into her attraction to him. If she started an affair with Michael, it would only complicate things more.

When Walt phoned on Wednesday to invite her out to a client's party, she knew it was the opportunity she'd been looking for to give her a break from thinking about work and her personal problems. She thought a night out with her old friend would give her the lift she needed. At least it would get her away from her house and the phone.

But the moment she opened the door that evening and the savvy investment broker gave her a brief but thorough once-over, she realized a few hours of light-hearted oblivion was wishful thinking.

"What hospital did you escape from?" he demanded, his benign smile turning into a scowl.

Blair tapped her nails against the solid wood door of her condominium and scowled back at the salt-and pepper-haired version of her favorite news anchorman. "Nothing like a friend to lift you up when you're feeling down."

"Down and out for the count from the looks of things. No wonder you've been hard to get a hold of lately. Listen," he drawled, sliding his hands into the pockets of his pin-striped Brooks Brothers suit, "we can forget this open house thing if you're feeling crabby."

Just for that Blair snatched up her purse and, elbowing him out of her way, shut her front door behind them. "I said we'd go, and we're going," she muttered, daring him with her narrowed eyes.

Pursing his lips, Walt followed her to his Cadillac. Once they were on their way and they'd exhausted small talk regarding the approaching dog days of summer and the current dip in the Dow Jones average, he shot her a sidelong look. "Am I going to get my head lopped off if I ask you what's happened?"

"Nothing's happened. As I told you on the phone, I've been busier than usual, that's all."

"Work used to get your adrenalin flowing, not turn you into a wraith."

"Can't I get tired like other human beings?"

"If that's what you are, sure. But I think it's something else, or more. If I didn't know you any better, I'd ask if you were having problems with your love life."

"Oh, thanks. Now it's impossible to conceive of me having a love life?"

Walt's stark eyebrows lifted a moment before he burst into laughter. "Well, I'll be damned. There *is* a man. Who is this guy who's finally hooked you?"

"No one, if I can help it."

"Doesn't look like it from where I'm sitting." Casting her another quick glance he made an abrupt turn into the hotel parking lot that housed his favorite lounge. "Never mind the party," he said, stopping before the valet parking sign. "You're going to tell brother Walt all about it."

It suddenly struck Blair that she wanted to. Her annoyance with him vanishing, she nodded mutely.

Minutes later they were settled in the dark, intimate lounge. A cocktail waitress took their order and quickly returned with their brandies. Taking the first sip, Blair groped for a way to begin.

"He's all wrong for me," she said at last.

"The worst kind to fall for. My ex-wife was the same way. I knew I should have run in the opposite direction the moment I saw her casing the jewelry counter at Neimans."

"He has ambitions of moving out to the boonies and growing bushes," she continued, ignoring his droll attempt at humor. "He thinks he can convince me that I want that, too."

Walt shot her a confused look. "Where'd you meet this guy? Is he a farmer friend of your mother's or something?"

"The corporate plant man."

"Pardon?"

Blair could hear the suspiciously unsteady timbre in his voice and warned, "Don't you dare laugh at me, Walter Sheffield. What was I supposed to do when you refused to escort me to my brother's wedding?"

"I'm not sure," the darkly tanned man replied, smoothing a finger over an eyebrow. "But I wouldn't have imagined this scenario in my wildest dreams. The guy who waters your office plants?"

"Don't be a snob," she sniffed. "He's very nice . . . and intelligent . . . plus I told you, he has ambitions."

"Good grief. No wonder you look ill—you've falling for the guy and you can't believe it, either!"

"Oh, Walt, what am I going to do?"

"Ask McGowan to open an office on the West Coast."

"Be serious. He's confusing my priorities, he's making me look back and wonder if I've been kidding myself about what I've been running away from all these years . . . but the problem with the whole thing is that I'm not sure I can trust him."

"You mean you think he might already be cheating on you?"

"You're a real morale-booster, you know that?"

"Blair, you know darned well that if Evelyn didn't already have her expensively manicured hands around my wallet and I didn't have the kids's college tuition to worry about, I'd chase you myself."

"No, you wouldn't. There's the small matter of my mother, remember?"

"I have a friend who's a travel agent. When things get too much for me, we could ship her off for an occasional world tour."

It was the kind of crazy response she knew she could count on from Walt and she reached across the table to squeeze his hand. "Thanks. Anyway, what I meant was that I keep getting these mixed signals from Michael." She told him about the would-be mugger and how Michael had stopped him; she told him about the gun in the glove compartment and the beeper. "And he never wants to talk about himself, unless it's about the nursery he wants to start. He encourages me to talk about my day, my life . . . am I going crazy or is there something strange in all that?"

"Lots of guys who were in the service know some basic martial arts moves—"

"Maybe, but I don't know if he's ever been in the service."

"—and if there were snakes the size you described out there, I'd sure want something to defend myself. Also, these days everyone's carrying beepers. As for his reticence . . ." Walt shrugged. "Can't you buy the idea that the guy's simply nuts about you?"

"I don't know," she admitted. "It would force me to face the issue of where this relationship is headed. Maybe I *am* tired of this insane pace my work demands, but what if it's only temporary? Anyway, moving away from Dallas is like swinging to the other extreme of the pendulum.''

''I suppose the question you have to ask yourself is, can you be happy without him in your life? Choices always demand trade-offs, you know that. Maybe you could work things out where you could start your own small agency—maybe McGowan and Birch would let you free-lance.''

''I love Dallas,'' she insisted fervently. ''I love city life.''

''Where did you say his place was? West of Tyler? That's not exactly Siberia, kiddo—and, by the way, do you know that when you were describing it to me a moment ago, your eyes lit up?''

''Just because it's a pretty place doesn't mean I want to migrate there,'' she replied, shrugging dismissively.

''If you say so.''

Blair downed the rest of her brandy and set it firmly on the table. ''On second thought, I'm tired of dwelling on my problems. Let's go to that party.''

Michael shifted to let the street lamp illuminate the face of his watch. Eleven-twenty. Ten minutes more, he told himself grimly. He would give her another ten minutes and then he was going home. He was beat, and he had to get up early in the morning. If he didn't get some rest, he was going to be worthless on the job. But seconds later when a car pulled into the driveway behind him, he straightened in his seat, his fatigue immediately forgotten.

Questions raced through his mind as he got out of his truck. Where had she been? Who was the guy she was with? What did he mean to her? But the moment she stepped from the silver Cadillac and, escorted by the middle-aged, sharply dressed man, circled toward him, he dismissed everything for the sheer relief of knowing she was safe.

The street light illuminated her pale face and her gorgeous dark eyes, watching him with that heart wrenching solemnity that would forever make him think of wary does and waifs. Her paleness was enhanced by her white crepe dress, lending her an ethereal quality, and he experienced a vicious spurt of jealousy before he forced it down. He wouldn't jump to conclusions. If he couldn't give her anything else, he would give her his patience.

"What are you doing here, Michael?" she asked quietly upon stopping before him.

"Waiting to see if you were all right. I've been calling throughout the evening and I was concerned."

"You had no reason to be."

Ignoring the mild censure in her voice, he extended his hand to the man beside her. "Michael Bishop."

"Walter Sheffield," Walt replied amiably. "Registered pacifist and primary supporter of two teenagers wanting to go to a hellishly expensive university."

Understanding that he clearly didn't want to be the cause of any trouble, Blair smiled wryly and, linking her arm with his, walked him back to his car. "Thanks for everything."

"I could stay."

"It isn't necessary."

"Then I'll be in touch." He glanced over her shoulder toward Michael who continued to watch them quietly.

Knowing why he was hesitating, Blair kissed his cheek and then stepped back from the car. She watched until he drove away before returning to Michael.

"Thank you for not making a scene," she told him, wondering if he could hear her heart pounding.

"I told you, I only wanted to make sure you were all right. It's difficult to do when you insist on refusing to take my calls or go out simply to avoid me."

"It wasn't simply to avoid you. Walt and I often attend business functions together."

"Because he's safe?"

"Because he's a friend."

Michael could hear the rising tension in her voice and took a deep calming breath. "I'm sorry. I don't want to argue with you. It's late and I know you're tired, so I'll be going."

That was *it*? Blair stared, completely stupefied. As he turned away she reached out without even thinking, touching his bare arm. He recoiled as if stung.

Blair shook her head, not knowing what to make of this retreat. "Michael . . . we have to talk."

"Not tonight."

"When?"

A good question, he thought bitterly. When things settled down at the Bureau? When he had his pension vested and he could quit? When he could convince his superiors that it wouldn't threaten security to tell her what he really was?

"I don't know," he said wearily.

The fatigue touched her more than anything, defeating her resolve and prompting her to step closer and tentatively touch his shoulder. He stiffened but didn't move away from her. Sensing some indescribable conflict within him, she laid her cheek against his back.

"Oh, Michael."

He closed his eyes in sweet agony. "You'd better go inside now, sweetheart. Because if you don't, I'm going to turn around and take what I'm aching for. Go on," he prompted, sensing her hesitation.

Though she stepped away from him, Blair continued to stand there for a moment longer. "I'm trying to understand you. Really I am."

Michael remained silent. After swallowing the lump that lodged in her throat, Blair stepped around him and did as he'd asked.

Chapter Nine

I'm sorry, Tess," Blair said, stopping her secretary as she read the letter just dictated. "Would you please read that last paragraph again?"

Glancing up from her steno pad, Tess gave her a concerned look before placing the pad in her lap and leaning forward in her chair. "Go after him," she said fervently. "I know what you're thinking—I gave him your message asking him to wait for you until you got out of this morning's meeting, and he left anyway. But maybe he had a good reason. Go after him and find out what it is."

"He didn't want to wait, isn't that clear enough?"

Tess stared at her friend, taking in the shadows under her eyes and her wan features that even a cheerful red suit couldn't brighten. "He looked preoccupied and about as drained as you do. Blair, something's dreadfully wrong here. Go talk to him!"

"How can I? We have the Raven Cosmetics people arriving in less than an hour, not to mention the Piazza luncheon I'm supposed to attend right afterward."

"Cosmetics . . . shopping malls—Blair, this is your life we're talking about here! Think of Pete Harkness—where did all his zealousness and ambition get him?"

Stunned at the younger woman's passionate outburst, Blair watched her walk out of the office. It was the heat, she told herself, resting her elbow on the arm of the chair to rub her forehead. The heat and the pressure. She was going to have to go to Roger McGowan and insist they hire some temporary staff, maybe even look into getting another ad executive. The workload was getting to be too much. But that didn't solve her immediate problem, namely, what to do about Michael.

"Oh, the devil with it," she muttered, rising and striding out of her office. Tess was busily rolling paper into her typewriter. "How long since he left?"

"Fifteen minutes at least. I'm sure he's up on six by now."

Six. Blair almost groaned out loud. She would give anything if she could avoid the sixth floor again. "Cover for me. I'll be back as soon as possible."

Luckily she didn't have to wait long for an elevator, but when it arrived she found herself face-to-face with several men. She recognized two as being dignitaries from one of the consulates upstairs. Two more had that ice-in-the-veins look of bodyguards, and the other could have stepped out of an El Greco painting.

"Excuse me," she said, deciding she would rather tackle the fire stairs than get into a car with this bunch. She beckoned them to go on. "I'll catch the next car."

"Please...there is room," El Greco said, holding the door open for her.

He might have an ascetic face, Blair thought with sinking spirits, but his eyes were twentieth century—direct and roving. Intuition told her his hands could be equally troublesome; not wanting to create a scene, Blair got in.

Silence seemed to pulsate during the one floor ride, as well as awkwardness when, upon their arrival, everyone waited for Blair to exit first. *She* would rather have deferred to them, thus choosing the opposite direction. However, she soon realized no one was going to budge until El Greco did, and he was waiting for her. Taking a gamble, she turned right. To her relief it was the correct choice and, as she hesitated at the end of the hall, she saw them go into the consulate at the opposite end of the building.

She exhaled the pent-up breath she'd been holding and was about to continue her search for Michael when he exited from the same consul. Carrying a large potted plant and his tray, he headed down the hallway. Not wanting to call out lest she attract more attention, Blair hurried after him.

She rounded the corner just in time to see him step inside the room at the end of the corridor. The janitorial washroom, she surmised, for she knew each floor had one in the same location. Quietly she followed.

The door was half-closed and as she peered around it, she could see he had his back to her, busy with lifting the clay pot out of its attractive brass planter. She was about to announce herself, but the words of greeting froze in her throat when she saw him take a small disc-like item from beneath the rag in his tray and attach it to the outside of the clay pot beneath the lip. Then he lowered it back into the brass planter.

Feeling a queasiness in her stomach, Blair had to swallow before she could speak. "Michael?"

He spun around. Though instinctively she knew he wouldn't ever physically hurt her, she couldn't help her defensive step backward.

"I . . . I didn't mean to startle you."

Michael quickly recovered his composure and gave Blair a wry smile that she noted didn't quite reach his eyes. "That's all right. I was only watering this."

But he hadn't put any water in it and one look at her eyes told him she knew it and had seen what he *had* done, as well. Knowing he had to try to cover his error for her own good, he pretended to realize his mistake and grimaced.

"Guess I'm so preoccupied with remembering to attach these new thermal monitors that I forgot half my job."

"Thermal monitor?" Blair glanced at the plant he placed back in the sink and watched him reach into his tray for one of the plastic jugs. She'd never heard of such a thing. It had looked more like a— No, she abruptly dismissed the thought, it couldn't be. Besides, what did she know of such things, except what she'd seen in the movies, and how factual could that be? "What's a thermal monitor?"

"Well, it's—ah—a gizmo that gauges the humidity in the air. We're testing it to see if it can be used to identify the best locations for different species of plants." He smiled again. This time it held boyish charm. "You don't want to hear about all that."

"Please go ahead—it's fascinating."

"It's also top secret. If my employer heard me telling you of its existence, I could be fired."

"Oh." Now that *did* sound like a TV melodrama. She glanced at the planter again, torn between wanting to believe him and wondering if he was playing her for a fool. "I wouldn't want you to do anything that would cost you your job, Michael."

His expression grew tender. "I know." But he also knew that every moment she stayed here complicated things, or could even place her in danger. Wanting nothing less than to draw her close and inhale the seductive scent that was uniquely hers, he forced himself to concentrate on getting her back downstairs. "What brings you up here?" he asked quietly.

He had to ask? Two days ago he'd been waiting for her at her condominium when she arrived home with Walt. Now it was Friday and when he'd come to her office on his rounds, he'd ignored her request to wait so they could talk. She was confused and she wanted some answers.

Michael could see what was going on inside her mind, but he felt helpless. Not only couldn't he explain, he didn't even have time to reassure her, not now when he'd been put on alert because it appeared something big was about to go down in one of the consulates.

Feeling as if he were being ripped in two, he dropped his gaze to the carpeted floor.

"I know you can't talk now, but could we meet later?" she asked, feeling more awkward by the minute. "This evening sometime?"

"I—Blair, I can't. I have to work. In a few days maybe—"

She gave a short, bitter laugh. "What is it, another thrip epidemic you have to conquer, or has the sprinkler system been acting up again? Damn it, Michael, if you've changed your mind about me, could you at least have the decency to say so? How am I supposed to make up *my* mind when I can't tell what *you* want from me?"

"This is what I want," he grated, reaching out and dragging her into his arms. "And this," he rasped, a heartbeat before he locked his mouth to hers.

Behind her closed lids Blair's world spun out of control. Her body went from chilled to feverish in seconds. Dear heaven, she wanted him so. There was no point in denying it any longer. She wanted him. Worse, she'd fallen in love with him. If that made her a fool, then so be it.

Accepting her heart's choice, she wrapped her arms tightly around his neck and responded with equal fervency to his kiss. It earned her an appreciative groan from Michael.

"Tonight," he whispered, pressing random kisses along her cheek and down her throat. "I don't know how late, but wait for me. Promise that no matter what, you'll wait up for me?''

Did he think she could sleep when the memory of his hot kisses burned in her mind? She caught his head between her hands and held it still so she could see his eyes. "And we'll talk, too?"

"Everything," he vowed, grasping her wrist and shifting her hand so he could press a kiss against her palm.

"Er—excuse me," a man in coveralls said peering around the door. "I hate to break up a party, but I need to get in here."

The building custodian, Blair thought, feeling Michael stiffen. *She* couldn't even bring herself to look at the man, she was so embarrassed.

"I'll wait," she whispered to Michael. Then she slipped past the man and hurried to the elevators.

The older man watched her until she disappeared around the corner before turning back to Michael. His sardonic expression turned hard.

"Of all the crazy stunts. Have you lost your mind, Bishop?"

My mind and my heart, Michael thought, and tonight he was going to straighten out the former, even if it cost him all the years he had vested with the Bureau, because one thing was for sure—nothing was worth the risk of losing Blair.

"Get out of my way, Dockery," he said, grabbing up the planter and pushing past the stocky man. "I have a plant to deliver."

Blair didn't know how she got through the hours afterward. It was past three by the time she returned to McGowan and Birch from her meeting with the Pi-azza group and, as she approached Tess's desk, she decided she needed to take the rest of the day off or else. But before she could tell her secretary as much, Tess hung up her phone, grabbed her purse and jumped to her feet.

"Never a dull moment," she told Blair in lieu of a greeting. "That was our illustrious office manager advising us we have to clear the building. A bomb threat has been called in to the building manager's office."

"Again?" Blair sighed. It seemed that someone was always phoning in a threat. Most of the time it was simply an unhappy applicant who'd been rejected for a mortgage loan by the firm upstairs, who was letting off steam. "Another unsatisfied customer."

"Uh-uh," Tess replied, falling in beside her to fol-low the rest of the staff already heading out the door. "One of our Latin American consulates is the target this time."

A cold hand gripped Blair's heart. No, she told herself, immediately rejecting the thought that popped into her mind. It couldn't be.

They followed the policy set down by the building's manager for such situations, exiting quickly but calmly by the fire stairs, then out the lobby to wait across the street or wherever they could find room. The area immediately in front of the building was jammed with people, so Tess and Blair headed far-ther up the street before crossing over.

"Rats, I think I forgot to turn off my typewriter," Tess said, glancing at her watch. "And Kent's supposed to call me and tell me if we're still on for the movies tonight."

"We'll probably be back upstairs within twenty minutes or so," Blair replied, as much to reassure herself as Tess. She shifted her purse and attaché case into her other hand and brushed her hair back from her face. "What's new with his sister? Was the report back to his parents favorable?"

The blonde smiled impishly. "You could say that. We're driving down to Austin to see them next month. After you get back from vacation, of course."

At the mention of vacation, Blair groaned. "I'm not sure I'm going to last that long. In fact, I was about to tell you I was taking the rest of the day off when you gave me this good news."

"You're going to meet Michael somewhere?" Tess asked hopefully.

"He's going to be tied up until later tonight, but I need a few hours alone to try to—".

Her mind went blank at the sight of him. She stared for several seconds, telling herself she was mistaken. It was too late in the day; he should have been gone hours ago. Yet she would recognize that shade of chestnut hair anywhere, that long lean build, those dark, intent eyes. He stood inside the doorway of another office building, watching the commotion across the street, occasionally lifting what looked to be a walkie-talkie to his lips.

A walkie talkie?

Cold dread rushed through Blair and in reaction she wrapped her arms around herself. Images, uninvited but vivid, flashed before her eyes...the day in the parking garage and another small radio-like device...the disc he'd attached to the planter this afternoon...the glasses...the locked doors...the secrets...*the gun*.

"Oh, God," she whispered.

Tess grabbed her arm. "Blair! What is it? You're as white as paste. Do you feel faint?"

She felt sick to her stomach, but she swallowed and forced herself to shake her head. "Let me go. There's something I have to do. I'll be all right," she insisted gently but firmly extricating herself.

He didn't see her until she was almost upon him and though he tried to hide the radio inside his windbreaker, one look at her face told him he would be wasting his time. Still, he receded another step into the protection of the doorway.

"You can't do this, Michael," she said upon stopping before him. She wasn't surprised to hear her voice shaking with emotion.

"You shouldn't be here. It's not safe. Go to your car and I'll see you later as I promised."

She opened her mouth to speak, but the words wouldn't come. Did he think they could go on as if nothing had happened, if he continued with this? She couldn't believe that she had been that wrong about him. She wouldn't. Grasping his sleeves she edged closer.

"I'll go. I'll even wait for you. But you have to turn yourself in."

"What?"

"Michael, I know. I know what you've done and I can't let you go through with it. Please, turn yourself into the police before it's too late. They might be more lenient if you do. I'll testify in your behalf."

She thought he was a terrorist. Michael didn't know whether to laugh or swear. She thought he was the person behind the bomb threat and she was trying to reform him. Even as he felt incredulous laughter rise to his throat, he wanted to crush her to him and kiss her breathless. You had to care deeply to risk that much. You had to love desperately.

He reached out to touch her cheek. "Sweetheart, everything's going to be all right. Just go on—"

"Will you stop!" she cried, pushing away his hand. She saw a policeman several yards away trying to keep curious onlookers from further crowding the area. "Turn yourself in, Michael, I beg you. If you don't, I will."

Great, Michael thought, that's all he needed. "Blair, I'm not turning myself in because I haven't done anything. Now, please—"

"Officer!"

As the uniformed patrolman came over, Michael did swear. "Honey, you don't know what a mistake you're making," he muttered.

"Yes, ma'am," the officer said, tipping his hat to Blair. "What seems to be the problem?"

"This man—this man—"

"Blair."

"He's the bomber," she blurted out. She took a deep gulp of breath. "He wants to t-turn himself in."

"Oh, hell," Michael muttered, reaching into his back pocket.

Instantly the officer took an offensive stance. "Freeze, buddy."

"It's all right, officer. I'm FBI. The name's Michael Bishop and I'm just reaching for my identification."

After a slight hesitation, the policeman nodded. "Do it slowly."

Blair watched in horror as Michael drew out the leather case and discreetly flipped it open. She was vaguely aware of the badge and the laminated card with his picture, but she saw it as if she were observing it from a great distance. In fact everything seemed to be drifting away, as if she were sliding down a deep tunnel.

"I'm working undercover and I'd appreciate if you'd allow me to keep it that way," Michael told the other man.

"No problem," he replied just as quietly. Then in a louder voice he added, "You folks will have to move from this doorway. It leads to the fire stairwell and if there's to be any more evacuating, we'll need this area cleared."

Michael nodded his thanks. "Of course, officer. Come on, darling. We'd better do as the man says." Pocketing his ID and shoving the radio inside his windbreaker, he grasped Blair's arm and directed her toward the parking garage.

Several yards away from the crowd, Blair jerked free.

"Don't cause a scene," he muttered. "As it is, I'm going to be in enough trouble for leaving my post."

"Then by all means, go back to your *post*."

Hearing the ice in her voice, Michael sighed inwardly. "I know what you must be thinking right now, but—"

"Oh, you can't begin to know."

"I never intended for this to happen."

"You mean you never intended for me to find out. You used me."

His answering laugh was abrupt. "That's rich. What were you doing when you first invited me to go to your brother's wedding and asked me to pretend I was a lawyer?"

"At least I warned you that I didn't have any ulterior motives. You lied to me. You pretended to care!"

They'd entered the garage and her voice echoed through the lower level. Michael winced, but it didn't stop him from grabbing her arm and swinging her around.

"I do care!"

"So much that you didn't trust me enough to tell me who you really were? God! The fool I made of myself. The torment I put myself through first believing that we were too different, then, when I began noticing all the inconsistencies, worrying what you really were and struggling to hold on to one redeeming *something* in you to believe in."

"Don't you think it killed me to have to keep the truth from you?"

"No. You people are trained to be good actors."

They'd arrived at her car and she blindly groped in her purse for her keys. Finding them she fumbled in her attempts to unlock the door. Michael snatched them from her hand and did it for her.

"See what I mean? Steady as a rock." She snatched the keys back and opening the door blindly tossed in her purse and case.

"You need time to get used to the idea. I'll call you later. As soon as this is over and I finish with my reports."

"I won't answer the phone."

"Then I'll come over."

"I won't let you in."

"I'm capable of letting myself in."

For a moment that unsettled her, but she quickly pulled herself together. "Don't you dare. Aren't you listening to anything I'm saying? I never want to see you again!"

The words came like a blow to the belly, but he managed to retain his calm outer shell and slowly nodded. "Maybe you feel that way right now, but when you've had time to think, you're also going to remember that you thought I was a bomber..." He edged closer so that their lips were only centimeters apart. "...and you still tried to save my neck."

"Knight One to Bishop. Do you copy?"

Blair, almost hypnotized by the passion in his eyes, recoiled as the message, garbled with static, came across his radio. "You'd better answer that, *Bishop.* Maybe Knight One has a client eager to invest in *thermal monitors.*"

Before he could reply she slid into her car, then slammed and locked the door. He had to jump out of the way when she jerked the car into reverse and shot out of her slot.

"Blair!" he shouted after her. "It's not over!"

It couldn't be. She had been ready to compromise herself to help him. He had to hold on to that.

"Bishop!"

"Yeah, yeah," he muttered to the impatient voice coming over the radio. But rather than reply he hurried back toward the crowd.

Chapter Ten

Here chick-chick . . . here chick. Wesley, stop that This here's for the chickens.''

Blair stood quietly at the back corner of her moth er's house watching her intermittently toss feed to th dozen chickens scurrying about and nudge her favor ite pig out of the way with her foot. The scene was on she'd witnessed dozens of times over the years, and th feeling of normalcy it gave her suddenly made her r alize this was why she'd come.

"Darn it all, Wes, will you stop? You're inhalin that stuff like you were a hog.''

"He is a hog, Mom.''

Woman and pig turned and in the next momer both were hurrying toward her. Blair knew that onl her mother was smiling, that Wesley's mouth alway had that dim-witted tilt to it, but just for a moment sh allowed herself to pretend, to bask in the welcome.

Martha Lawrence set her feed pail on a fence post and extended her bony, sun-freckled arms. She wore a faded blue-and-gray print housedress that had been shapeless even before its numerous washings, and her hair was still damp from her shower. As Blair hugged her, kissing her finely wrinkled cheek, she was acutely aware of the marks of time on her mother; the delicacy of her bones despite the energetic embrace; the silver and gray hair that was quickly replacing the once sandy blond, fine curls. It caused a burning in Blair's eyes and, in an attempt to hide it from her, she bent to pat the red pig sniffing her Italian sandals.

"Hello, Wes, you big hunk of bacon. Don't even think of nibbling on those. Where's Wanda?"

"In the shed with her babies. Wes snatched her share of squash bread a while ago and she's sulking. What's wrong with you?"

Leave it to her mother not to miss a thing and get straight to the heart of a matter, Blair thought wryly. Straightening, she brushed her hands together and considered the rose-covered trellis, gilded with gold by the light of the descending sun. The lighting had been almost identical when she and Michael had stood there a few weeks ago.

"Why does something have to be wrong for me to visit you?"

"Because it's Friday night and there's a thousand and one things a pretty, single girl should be doing instead of visiting her mother. And because I called your office after I heard about the bomb scare on the radio and Tess said you never came back to the office."

"It was already late and I decided there was no sense to try to get any more work done."

"She said she saw you with Michael, that you two were walking away together, and you seemed to be upset."

Blair pursed her lips. "I hate it when you two gang up on me."

"So you *were* upset?" When her daughter rolled her eyes, Martha Lawrence slipped her arm around her waist and directed her toward the house. "Let's go inside. I'll pour you a glass of sherry and you can tell me about it."

"You know I hate sherry, and I don't want to discuss Michael."

"Of course you do, dear. Otherwise you wouldn't have come."

Minutes later Blair found herself sitting at the kitchen table with a three-quarter-filled wineglass of her mother's cure-all. Martha Lawrence, having opened herself a can of beer, stood at the kitchen sink seemingly preoccupied with the task of shelling peas and preparing them for canning. Knowing she would only get a lecture on being wasteful if she didn't drink the liqueur, Blair took an initial sip and allowed a philosophical shrug.

"I guess it's not too bad," she muttered.

"Your taste buds are maturing. Remember when you hated blue cheese dressing? Of course, what I never told you was it was your father's favorite dressing and that it took me years before I developed a taste for it, too. He always insisted on calling it Roquefort, even if the stuff came out of a bottle and was manufactured in Pittsburgh. He had such airs, your daddy did—always dreaming of bigger and better, and always cutting his ties with what didn't work out to suit him. Is that what you're trying to do with Michael?''

Blair stared at her mother for several long seconds. The cheerful sound of pea pods popping and being dropped into a stainless steel pot were a comical accompaniment to such a dramatic revelation. No soulful violins or haunting oboes in this family, she thought dryly. Life with the Lawrences always seemed much the same as a Woody Allen picture.

''There's no comparison between us, Mother,'' she said stiffly. ''And I resent the suggestion that I'm taking after him.''

''Babydoll, as much as I think you prefer the idea, I didn't have you by Immaculate Conception, and I wasn't suggesting that you're a chip off the old block. But facts are facts—you're his daughter as much as you are mine.''

''I'm my *own* person and the choices I make in life are based on justification, not genes.''

Martha Lawrence's pace never faltered. ''So you've 'justified' yourself into pushing Michael away, is that what you're saying?''

''Will you stop defending him when you have no idea what he's done! Mother, he's not the simple, uncomplicated man you think he is. He's an FBI agent, and he used me. He's been working undercover for heaven knows what reason, and he decided a liaison with a woman in the building would authenticate the scenario.''

''Is that what he told you?''

"Of course not. He made the appropriate protestations about how he had no choice in deceiving me, how his hands were tied and how he thought he was protecting me. Ha! You know what I think? I think he needed a backup excuse to get into the building more often and I was handy. God, what a fool I was. I actually started to believe in him. I was torturing myself in a debate over my career and how to fit it in with his dreams of starting a wholesale nursery in east Texas."

"Whoa!" Martha Lawrence dropped the pod she'd been holding back into the sink and wiped her hands on her apron. Picking up her beer, she took a quick swallow and crossed over to take the seat beside Blair. "Suppose you back up some and tell me this story from the beginning."

Minutes later Blair paused to soothe her dry throat with a sip of sherry. She cast a wary glance at her mother, who'd remained silent throughout her explanation and now sat with her head bowed, turning the beer can round and round between her hands.

"Well?" she said when she couldn't take the silence any longer. "Say something."

Martha Lawrence's only reaction was a slight, albeit suspicious twitch in her shoulders.

"Mother!"

The older woman burst into laughter. "I'm sorry," she wheezed, reaching into her pocket for a tissue to wipe her tearing eyes. "That's the funniest thing I've heard in ages. You mean to tell me that you first asked him to come to the wedding pretending that he was a lawyer and all the while he was pretending to be a—what did you call him?—corporate plant man? That's as entertaining as any story line on my afternoon soap. You know the one I'm always telling you about? Topaz was trying to impress Reeve by going out with her tycoon boss, Linc, but instead they ended up—''

"For heaven's sake, Mama, this is real life, not some soap opera!" Blair cried, addressing her mother in a way she hadn't since the days when they found themselves in a joint struggle to make ends meet.

It wasn't lost on the other woman who, though she managed to stop laughing outright, shook her head and smiled wryly. "What do you want me to say?" she asked patiently. "So the man kept a secret—well, you started with a lie. From where I'm sitting that evens things out. The thing you should be concentrating on now is whether or not you're making a big mistake in wanting to throw away all those feelings that have grown between you two."

Blair fingered the rim of her wine glass. "It would never have worked out anyway," she mumbled. "My work is in Dallas and he wants to move out to the country. Can you see me going back to that sort of life?" she added with an awkward laugh.

"I don't know. You might be successful but you aren't happy with the way things are now. Blair, you know what your trouble is? You've got a severe case of tunnel vision. When are you going to stop comparing all men with your daddy? Yes, he hurt us and, yes, it was tough. But just because he left me doesn't mean your man's going to let you down."

Tears swelled in Blair's eyes. "Didn't Daddy know how much we needed him, Mom? Didn't he know how much we loved him?"

Martha Lawrence sighed and gripped her daughter's smooth hand within her own. "I don't know, baby. Maybe he did, but maybe he just didn't have anything to give back. Either way, it's time to let go. It's time to stop using his mistake to avoid taking risks yourself."

"I'm not sure I can let myself trust Michael again."

"He gave you another chance after that farce you put him through, didn't he? You do the same and I don't think you'll go wrong."

"Oh, Mom..." Blair slipped out of her chair and kneeling on the linoleum floor, laid her head in her mother's lap. "You must think I'm such a ninny."

Martha Lawrence blinked back her own tears and lovingly stroked her daughter's hair. "Only once in a while, dear, but you know it's a relief, too. How else can I justify my meddling?"

Blair chuckled, then sniffed. "Don't ever stop, okay?"

"I want that in writing."

It was almost midnight when Blair finally returned to her condominium. She'd stayed with her mother to help her finish shelling the peas, and they talked of the past in a way they never had before. Blair doubted she would ever achieve the philosophical outlook toward her father that her mother had, but tonight she'd taken a big step in letting go of the bitterness.

After emptying her mailbox, she let herself in through the front door. Knowing her mother wouldn't rest comfortably unless she knew Blair had arrived home safely, she turned on the light by the phone, dialed her number and gave her the two ring code they'd developed years ago. Then she hung up and checked the messages on her answering machine.

One was from Tess, one was from her mother—obviously before she'd arrived at the farm—and three were from Michael. Just hearing his low, entreating voice made her knees weak with longing and knotted her insides. She drew her fingertips across the machine as if it were his face, wishing it wasn't so late. She wasn't sure what the future held for them, but at the least she wanted to apologize for the way she'd spoken to him.

If he feels half as bad as you do, he won't be able to sleep. Call him.

She reached for the phone again—and stood there.

She didn't have his number.

Exhaling her frustration she slipped out of her jacket and headed down the hallway toward her bedroom. Maybe he would call again, she told herself. Maybe she would test the theory about phones and tubs and run a bath. At any rate it might help her relax. She certainly wasn't going to fall asleep in the state she was in.

Something white on the carpet caught her attention just outside her bedroom. She stooped to pick it up, rubbing it between her fingers. A flower petal, she realized lifting it to her nose. Gardenia. She often kept a vase of flowers in her room and had replaced a bouquet only this morning. But there wasn't a gardenia among the blossoms.

A few feet away was another petal and beyond it another. Blair's heart began to pound. Straightening, she stepped into the dark room following the trail to her bed. There on the dark print bedspread were several more creamy white petals and, laying in the center of them, a perfect gardenia.

Her hand was trembling, but she picked it up and lifted it close to draw in its exotic scent. "Oh, Michael," she whispered.

"Is that an 'Oh, Michael' you like it, or an 'Oh, Michael' how dare I break into your home?"

She gasped and spun around the moment he began to speak and now stared at him as he stood in the shadows, leaning against her closet door, his arms crossed over his chest. She lowered the hand she'd clapped to her mouth to her throat and groaned.

"I hate it when you do that."

"I thought once you saw the petals and the flower you'd know it was me."

"No—yes. But I thought you'd gone. There's no car outside."

"I asked Harry to drive me over. I thought if you saw my truck out front, you might not come in."

"How *did* you get in?"

"The sliding glass door in the back."

She nodded and lowered her gaze to the gardenia, not sure what to say next. She could feel his eyes moving over her, but she couldn't tell what he was thinking or what he wanted. Had this gesture just been his way of saying goodbye?

"I—um—I saw the news on TV at my mother's. I know about there really being a bomb in the consulate, and that it had been dismantled. Do you think they arrested all of the people from the radical group who were protesting that visiting official?"

Michael lifted one shoulder. "The ones who'd followed him to the States this time. Next time, who knows?"

"I rode up in the same elevator with him. He wasn't wearing a uniform, otherwise I might have recognized him from other news clips."

"The meeting was supposed to be a secret, that's why they chose Dallas and the consulate. Everything seemed to be going well until late afternoon. Somehow they managed to get the bomb on the cart sent up with coffee."

"You'd suspected something like that could happen for a while, hadn't you?" she asked, thinking back. "That's why you'd been doing surveillance. That disc, was it what I think it was?"

Michael inclined his head. "It paid off, too. We learned that the receptionist was a member of the group that planted the bomb."

Blair tried to take it all in, but all she could focus on was that he could have been killed. It made her shiver and she wrapped her arms protectively around herself.

Seeing her reaction, Michael's hopes plummeted. He'd thought if he explained she might accept the explanation and they could try again. But how could he ask her to ignore her repulsion to his work?

"Do you want me to leave?"

"No!"

He pushed away from the closet door needing to see if her eyes affirmed what he'd heard in her voice. "I never used you," he said quickly. "And I would never have let anything happen to you."

"I think I know that now."

It was barely a whisper, but he heard it. He took another step closer and then a final one until only inches separated them. Her face was pale and her eyes looked slightly swollen, as if she'd been crying. Lifting a hand, he drew his thumb across her high cheekbone. "I love you. You'll have to live with that. I'll try not to rush you...I'll try to give you the time and space you need..."

"Michael." She smiled through her tears. "You talk too much."

Not sure he wasn't dreaming, he framed her face with his hands, then slowly lowered his mouth to hers. She answered the gentle pressure with eagerness and, groaning, he swept her tightly against him.

The kiss was a frenzied claiming, a bittersweet communion. It telegraphed feelings long suppressed and needs denied, until soon they were breathless and trembling against one another. But neither made a move to let go.

"Say it," he whispered rocking his forehead against hers. "I want to hear you say it."

"I love you."

"Thank God. I thought I blew it."

"No, I almost did," she admitted, lowering her eyes shyly at his bemused look. "I've been doing a lot of thinking this afternoon, and I talked to my mother."

"Remind me to give her a big kiss next time I see her. What did she say?"

"She reminded me that I'd developed a tunnel vision regarding relationships, labeling anything lasting as futile because of my bitter memories of my father. I realized how unfair I was being by judging you on the basis of what he'd done. I condemned you for not trusting me enough to tell me who you really were, while all the time *I* was being a hypocrite because I wasn't willing to trust *you* to prove you were different."

"You've had quite a night," he murmured, stroking her hair.

"But when I think of how it could have turned out—"

"Shh." Lightly touching his index finger to her lips, he smiled down at her. "That's behind us. Tomorrow I'm going to my superiors and ask for a desk job. No, don't look at me that way. This has been coming for a while—since I lost my closest friend. He had a family and he was talking about doing the same thing, but there was always one more case. I'm not going to make that mistake, and I won't miss the field if I know I have you to come home to every night."

She shook her head in disbelief. "You would do that for me?"

"I told you, I love you. I would do anything for you, even stay in Dallas after I retire from the Bureau if that's what it will take to make you happy."

It was humbling to think he would walk away from everything he'd worked for out of love for her, and she realized with a stunning clarity what a generous thing loving was. "Well, I don't know," she began whimsically. "I think I could be pretty happy living in that field where the wildflowers grow."

This time it was Michael's turn to shake his head. "Wait a minute, what about your work?"

"I can still work," she replied, remembering something Walt had said to her. "There is such a thing as free-lancing, you know. We'll talk about it, but I think I like the idea of our children growing up seeing deer outside their bedroom windows."

It almost hurt, Michael thought, tightening his arms around her. Knowing there was only one antidote that would relieve the sweet ache, he claimed her mouth with his. Blair eagerly parted her lips and when he stroked his tongue against hers, she repeated the caress with equal ardor. Soon there was no more need for words. They found a language based solely on touch that was far more communicative.

As Michael lowered Blair to the petal-covered bed, they smiled into each other's eyes, remembering another time when they'd been this close. Blair caressed his cheek with the blossom in her hand. No longer did his intent look unsettle her. She only counted her blessings that she'd realized in time to cherish this special man.

"Don't ask me to leave tonight," he whispered, nibbling at her lips as he gazed deeply into her eyes.

"I don't want you to."

"We'll get our license in the morning."

"Fine."

"Your mother can even come along."

As if in reply, the phone rang once, twice, and then there was silence. Michael lifted his head and gave her an odd look.

"Who do you suppose that was?"

"My mother saying message received and understood."

"Huh?"

"Never mind," Blair chuckled, drawing his head down toward hers. "I'll explain later."

*   *   *   *   *

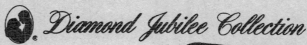 *Diamond Jubilee Collection*

It's our 10th Anniversary... and *you* get a present!

This collection of early Silhouette Romances features novels written by three of your favorite authors:

ANN MAJOR—*Wild Lady*
ANNETTE BROADRICK—*Circumstantial Evidence*
DIXIE BROWNING—*Island on the Hill*

* These Silhouette Romance titles were first published in the early 1980s and have not been available since!

* Beautiful Collector's Edition bound in antique green simulated leather to last a lifetime!

* Embossed in gold on the cover and spine!

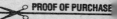 **PROOF OF PURCHASE**

This special collection will not be sold in retail stores and is only available through this exclusive offer:

Send your name, address and zip or postal code, along with six proof-of-purchase coupons from any Silhouette Romance published in June, July and/or August, plus $2.50 for postage and handling (check or money order—please do not send cash) payable to Silhouette Reader Service to:

In the U.S. Free Book Offer Silhouette Books 901 Fuhrmann Blvd. Box 9055 Buffalo, NY 14269-9055	**In Canada** Free Book Offer Silhouette Books P.O. Box 609 Fort Erie, Ontario L2A 5X3

(Please allow 4-6 weeks for delivery. Hurry! Quantities are limited.
Offer expires September 30, 1990.)

DJC-1.

Take 4 bestselling love stories FREE

Plus get a FREE surprise gift!

Special Limited-time Offer

Mail to   **Silhouette Reader Service®**

In the U.S.	In Canada
901 Fuhrmann Blvd.	P.O. Box 609
P.O. Box 1867	Fort Erie, Ontario
Buffalo, N.Y. 14269-1867	L2A 5X3

YES! Please send me 4 free Silhouette Romance® novels and my free surprise gift. Then send me 6 brand-new novels every month, which I will receive months before they appear in bookstores. Bill me at the already low price of $2.25* each. There are no shipping, handling or other hidden costs. I understand that accepting these books and gifts places me under no obligation ever to buy any books. I can always return a shipment and cancel at any time. Even if I never buy another book from Silhouette, the 4 free books and the surprise gift are mine to keep forever.

* Offer slightly different in Canada—$2.25 per book plus 69¢ per shipment for delivery.

Sales tax applicable in N.Y. and Iowa.   315 BPA 8176   (CAN)

215 BPA HAVY (US)

Name   (PLEASE PRINT)

Address   Apt. No.

City   State/Prov.   Zip/Postal Code

COMING SOON...

For years Harlequin and Silhouette novels have been taking readers places—but only in their imaginations.

This fall look for PASSPORT TO ROMANCE, a promotion that could take you around the corner or around the world!

Watch for it in September!

★